Eli

A local story told by a local writer! Enjoy

Grandma Rae

America Bound

The Journey West

Written and illustrated by

Jan Smith

Acknowledgments

    To my husband Bruce who patiently allowed me to sit hours at a computer doing uninterrupted research, writing and endless rewriting to complete this story. His willingness and ability to edit and critique are a blessing few wives who are authors have the honor of experiencing.

    To my parents and grandparents Nordic ancestry that inspires me and draws me into researching the early mythology of Odin, the life of the kings and their *thralls* or servants, and the religious and economic reasons they left the Old Country for a land of milk and honey and a richer life.

The most salient facts, events and circumstances set forth in this book are the events related to crossing from the upper Nordic mountains in Europe to the New World (the United States) and settling in the Northwest Territory on what is now Minnesota and North Dakota, separated by the Red River of the North. The work is historical fiction, enhanced by the actual events so documented through extensive research of the wagon trains crossing from the east coast over the mountains to Carver's Cove, St. Paul Minnesota today, and the early oxcart trails from there to the Red River and the territory north from there, Old Crossing or Georgetown, Minnesota today. Elaborations to enhance readability do not compromise any main truths.

Preface

Life in the Scandes, the Nordic Mountains in Norway, in the late 1700's meant living on a *bard*, a small (twenty-five acres or so) tract of land, owned by an individual who answered to a king. A commoner and his family subsisted on whatever the owner allowed them to keep. Often that meant the most meager of meals, clothing and shelter. One can only imagine the courage, determination and fears our forefathers felt when and one of the family made the decision to leave the Old Country and come to the New World. America was pictured as a land of *milk and honey*. Each who left dreamed of owning land or a small business and being respected for that endeavor.

AMERICA BOUND historically tells the story of a young man and his desire to come to the New World. Having little *penger* (money), he works his way from his home in the Nordic Mountains to the Red River of the North located on the edge of what was then the Northwest Territory or the Eastern Dakota Territory in search of his Uncle Olaf who he hopes will help him fulfill his dreams. Each day is a new learning experience, fostered by trial and error, heartache and happiness as he deals with life on the Domino, wagon and oxcart trails, the Native Americans he meets and the likes of Scratch, Pig's Eye, Mart's daughter, Okomisan, River and Feather.

Chapter 1

    Sunlight spread its radiance over the slopes of the far off Nordic Scandes mountainside, across a stream that separated Bjorn as he herded the sheep from the rest of the *gard* owned by Jacob Israelson. Eighteen years old and considered an adult by Nordic standards, he was content, as content as one could be knowing he'd never own land. Far (father) was head *husman* for Israelson. As chief hired man, Far saw that the other five *husmen* completed the tasks Israelson assigned each day.
    For part of his father's wages for being head *husman*, Erik, Bjorn's older brother, Mor (mother), young sister Anna and Bjorn subsisted on one-quarter acre of

land supplied by Israelson. Home was a small, one room hut or daub house made by weaving wood and vines into a frame. A mixture of sand and grass as a sealant from the wind and rain coated the inside walls. The thatched roof cut from shingled bark off the trees that served as support for the wood beams of the roof didn't leak, a comfort to all of them when those rains came in torrents across the mountain. A fireplace served as heat on cold nights and a cooking fire each day, occupying the wall that was part of the hillock. Four rope beds, all covered with a ticking mattress stuffed with grass, hung on each side of the fireplace, attached to the sturdy poles that supported the roof. A hand hewn wood table with five chairs sat just inside the door and in front of shelving along one wall that held the cooking pots, meager staples for meals, and any extra clothing.

To live on the *gard's* land meant that the four of them worked a specified number of days for Israelson, whenever and wherever he needed their help. They parceled out any produce grown on their meager acreage and handed over to him his due, according to the agreement Far made when he first came to work for Israelson. Mor's herb garden yielded well with her tender caring. She trekked weekly to market with her leftover allocation to sell her share of the herbs. With those funds, she bartered and bought family necessities.

Israelson's *gard* consisted partially of the flat and gently sloped land at the base of the Scandes on one side of a river. The crops planted each year supplied most of the family's needs. His 25 acres of field land on this side were one of the largest holdings in this Nordic area and five *husman* families tended them. He'd divided his 10 more acres across the river and on the opposite mountainside into three *stols* or *seters*, small two to three acre plots suitable for grazing animals.

Each *stol* or *seter* had its purpose. The *stol* furthest up the mountain side had three huts that served as summer living quarters for his *husmen* or women he assigned to stay there. One hut held the curing cheese, another was the herdsmen's hut and a third, more a simple shelter, was available for anyone needing a place to stay for the night. Spring meant that ewes producing milk occupied this *seter* and Stina, the *seterjente* (dairymaid) spent her days here, milking the ewes twice a day. She made the best cheese in this Nordic region. When Stina's *ost hus* (cheese house) was full and the cheese cured well, a flag flew on the hut, high enough so it was visible at the *gard*. Erik came across the river with cart and horse to take it to market. Stina's Cheese, as it was known at market, sold out quickly each time Erik made the trip.

Stina loved the solitude of the *stol* and contentedly milked the ewes and made the cheese when the time was right. The aroma of her bread baked each day on the flat stones floated on the windswept mountainside and strangers often stopped for a sampling. Her clever sheep dog that faithfully chased wolves and warned of intruders added to the peacefulness that she felt here at the *stol*.

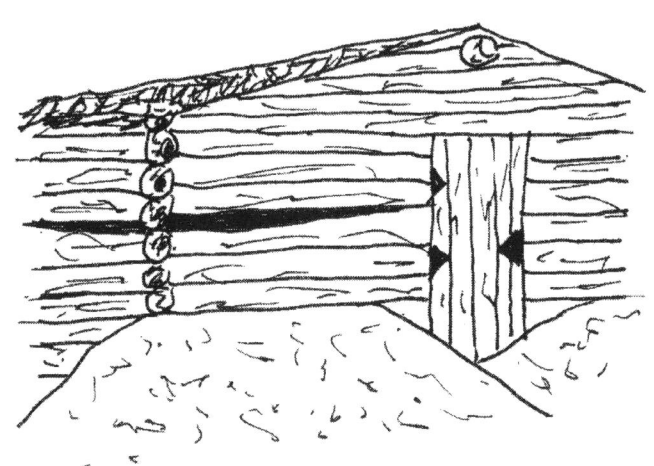

When he saw the flag fly as he sat gazing out across the river and above him for any unusual activity, Bjorn was happiest. It's flapping in the wind meant he'd have a visitor from home. Bjorn's *stol* was not as far up the mountainside as the *ost hus stol* was. He never felt neglected by the family for two reasons. The lambs, recently weaned from their mothers, were a noisy lot but loving, always looking for the attention lost by the separation from their mother's side. Erik always stopped for a time on his way back from the *ost hus* and brought news from the family and a loaf of Mor's bread. Visits from Eric were special since Bjorn rarely got back to the family home during weaning season. "Better being assigned here to watch the sheep than other chores I do when the lambs are yearlings," he often voiced. The responsibility of caring for the sheep was far less labor intense than wrestling with horse and plow, logging, or expecting to wield a sword if the King requested men at arms from Israelson's *husmen*.

Sleeping in a make-shift small one-room hut built into the mountainside, nestled on a ledge at the top of this *stol's* plot of land was in a way comforting for Bjorn. The family's trials caused by lack of money and space didn't affect him here. The height of the mountainside afforded him a view of the valley spread out below him and across the river. The trail up to his *stol* was very visible and provided fair warning when someone came to visit.

Poaching was uncommon in this Nordic region, but one never knew when the wolves would come and cause trouble. Shep and Beck, the two trained sheep herding dogs, kept the lambs corralled on the three acre parcel and were his dependable buddies.

Each member of Bjorn's family, except for Anna, his five year old sister, had responsibilities. Bjorn found his assigned duty of watching the flock of sheep spread out in front of him enjoyable on days like this when the sun shone and warmed his bones. Looking across today, he saw his Far, Hans, behind a horse and plow, fallowing the oat field just harvested. Mor was in the garden. When she wasn't tending the small plot, she did "house" duty when visitors came to the *gard*.

Erik never knew what he'd do each day and found himself sent off wherever Israelson needed strong, swift legs to run or sensible hands to drive the horse and cart. That was the case today. Israelson saw the flag flying and ordered Erik to get the cheese and take it to market.

The third *stol* on a grassy slope with a little more acreage was the farthest down the mountainside, closer to the *gard* and the river. Israelson's cattle grazed on this plot all summer. Another *husman* watched over them as Bjorn did the sheep.

Chapter 2

Bjorn's dream was to own a *Burk*, one of the smaller farmsteads in the area that sometimes were for sale. To earn enough money, even for a down payment, was probably impossible for him. Earning enough to pay for passage to the New World was more probable in his own mind. "I've already saved the equivalent of half of the ship passage fee or $10. All I need is $8 more for the ticket." He thought a while and decided, "I'll need more *penger* (money) to get myself from the ship's port to Carver's Cove (today St. Paul) on the Mississippi." He hoped to join an oxcart train there, headed for Old Crossing (Georgetown MN today). Olaf, Mor's uncle, lived near the Red River of the North located on the edge of the Northwest Territory or the Eastern Dakota Territory.

The New World beckoned many second sons like Bjorn, eager to be self-sufficient and able to establish their own families. Bjorn did not have a *kjaereste* (sweetheart) like Erik did. He knew girls that were marrying age, but Bjorn had no time or opportunity to court one of them. He had nothing to promise if he did. Away from the *gard* most of the time herding the sheep, tending the fields or fighting in the Kind's guard left him with little time to be with the family and less free time to seek a helpmate.

Bjorn dreamt of settling somewhere – staking out a portion of land in the New World's lush country, living on it for the time needed to care for it until it could be his. "I'll send *penger* home so Mor and Far won't have to work so hard. Maybe Anna can go to school when she's old enough," he voiced, aware there was no one around to hear him or so he thought. Erik's visual presence on the mountainside above lightened his spirits.

"Bror!" Bjorn spoke and waved, trying not to shout so that what he said echoed across the region. "How are you, Bror, and how is the family?"

"Tired, but well," came the answer once Erik was closer.

"Did Stina give you a slice or two of *ost* for me?"

"She gave me more than a slice. Here's a round. You sweet on her?" Erik questioned, digging in his knapsack to retrieve the generous portion wrapped in a white homespun cloth.

"*Nei*, (no) but I've been thinking, Bror. Remember the letter we got from Uncle Olaf?"

"*Ja*, (yes) about the Indians looting the oxcart and stealing his chickens when he was getting water from the Red? *Hvorfor* (Why)?"

"Up here, I have lots of time to think."

"You're not leaving are you? That land calling you? Calls me too, Bror. Maybe we should both go."

"You?" Bjorn answered in a surprised voice. "Why would you leave? You're the oldest. What's left when Mor and Far pass on will be yours."

"And what'll that be? You know they own nothing. A few clothes. Some pots. Not even a horse. Mor's chickens she cares for aren't even hers. What's here for me?"

"Selma," answered Bjorn with a smile on his face. "She comes from good stock."

"*Ja*, and she's the only thing that will keep me here. But you – how will you get the *penger* for the ticket?"

"I have half of it now. I'm promised one of the lambs if I don't lose any to the wolves. I'll sell that at market. That should get me to the fjord where the ships leave. I'll sign on and work my way as a deck swabber if I have to."

"You're serious, aren't you? So you get on a ship. Get to the New World. Then what?" questioned Erik with concern on in his voice. "How will you get the rest of the way over the mountains to this new territory that is in the middle of that country as I understand it?"

"More work. There are oxcart and wagon trains that leave daily for this New Territory. I can handle horses. Herd livestock if that's a choice. Once I am in Carver's Cove, I'll sign on with one of the trains. Olaf said that driving oxen is like driving a stubborn old nag that doesn't want to work. Remember? Can't be any worse than trying to farrow the land with that old horse of Israelson's."

"Think about this some more. We'll talk again." Erik rose. "I have to go and get this cheese to market. Already wasted too much time. I'll be an hour later than usual."

"Won't matter. Her cheese will go in a flash. You know that."

"*Ja*, but I need to get back to the *gard* too so Mor doesn't worry."

"*Tukk* (thanks) for stopping."

Reaching the horse and cart, he turned suddenly and said, "Forgot to tell you. When the lambs are ready, you're to report to the King's guard. King's determined to control that land north of here, along the coast. He's looking to raise an army to do so. Israelson's ordered to send men." With that, Erik, horse and cart disappeared around a trail bend and wound their way down the mountainside.

Chapter 3

Leaving the family was heart-wrenching. Bjorn had to make so many decisions as each new day dawned. When he couldn't find a cart going to the harbor, he walked the well-worn trail that people along the way told him would eventually reach the landing where the ships to the New World moored. The mountain runoff became the trail Bjorn followed to get to the harbor. It meandered downstream from Israelson's *gard* until it met the Nidelva River that flowed into Trondheimsfjorden where ships docked.

The recently unloaded barge he boarded on the Nidelva moved slowly as it manipulated the bends and curves, the deadheads and huge boulders that had rolled off the mountainsides. Negotiating with Henson, the barge operator, for a free fare meant loading and unloading barrels, crates, produce, and sometimes even animals at each stop along the way. Working for his passage kept *"penger"* in Bjorn's pocket and gave him a little extra too.

He had no idea when the next ship to the New World would sail or if he could find work aboard it. Any way he could avoid paying for food, lodging, or transportation stretched his meager resources. If he had to pay the $18 for his passage on the schooner, he'd need cash left once he got to the New World.

The numbers of wild animals along the twisting and turning of the river between stops to load and unload surprised him and kept him entertained. Otters along with their friends the beaver, whose dams were part of the navigational hazards, frolicked and played along the shore. Badgers and foxes scrounging dinner along the banks were common sightings. Closer to Trondheimsfjorden, moose and deer grazed on the gentle slopes of the hills. Bjorn watched them wander down to the water's edge and drink. "These are the young ones born this year, rejected by their mothers," he decided.

Reaching the harbor, Bjorn helped unload the wool and cheese Israelson had placed on the barge to sell. Reloading the flour barrels, the seed needed for planting the *gard*, a new plowshare, and other smaller crates whose contents were not marked took longer. Henson made sure the freight was well tied down for the trip back up the Nidelva.

"*Tukk* (thanks) for all your help. You sure you won't consider working for me?" asked Henson. "The last schooner that sailed out of here never came back. Most likely was lost in that storm we had not long ago – the one that flooded the shipyard with its tremendous wave action. Destroyed some of the boats and some of the docks."

"Grateful for your offer – more grateful for the free passage. I know it's risky but I have a dream like many my age. I've no responsibilities. This is the time for me to strike out on my own and see if I can get to where there is land for the taking. My family barely survives after Israelson's paid. Hope I can help them in some way." Bjorn shook Henson's hand and made his way to the schooner in port that was loading for morning departure to New World.

Chapter 4

Trondheimsfjorden harbor, calm and sheltered, protected the city proper from the ever-present winds that blew due to the mountainous terrain. Bjorn looked at the buildings facing him built into the base of the mountainside. "Ship's Wheel. There it is," announced Bjorn to no one, but assured himself he'd found the address where he was to see about passage aboard the Domino. He walked the short way over the wood planking to the inn.

Opening the door, a raucous noise greeted him. Smoke from the hearth stung his eyes. The only people in the inn were the three men that stood in line in front of a table in the corner and the inn keeper. "Must be the ship's captain," thought Bjorn, so he got in line too.
His turn came and the captain looked him over good. "Ever worked on a schooner before, Laddie?"
"*Nei*, but I'm willing to do most anything and I learn fast," Bjorn replied.

"Ever sailed on a three-masted rig like the Domino before?"

"*Nei*, never sailed," answered Bjorn, looking the captain straight in the eyes. "Herded sheep in the mountains most of my life. I'm a second son and hope to make my way to the New Territories in the New World north of Carter's Cove and claim some of that free land."

"Nothing's free, son. Mark my word. You'll pay along the way." The captain leaned back on the back legs of his chair, undecided what to do about this new, well-muscled recruit with no sailing experience. Bjorn kept a steady gaze into the face of the captain all the while. "Tell you what – agree to swab the upper decks and my cabin morning and night, watch and obey Scratch's commands and I'll sign you on with free passage."

"Who's Scratch?"

"Like you, boy. Like a person who checks out the details before agreeing. Scratch is my mast man. Been with me since I became captain on this rig. He makes sure each time those sails go up and down that they've been stowed correctly, that the roping doesn't tangle during use. More importantly – that they're ready for the next time they're needed. We have oars aboard. When there's no wind which is seldom, we break them out and row. I'll expect you to use those muscles I see and take your turn rowing. Doesn't happen often. We have deadlines to meet on shipments, Laddie, so we keep moving by wind or hard labor until we reach our destination. Ship has fore and aft bulkheads. I'll draw you a picture and point out where they are. Helps to know a little about the lay of the ship."

Scratch will show you around when you get on board and where the sails are that you'll help hoist.

Reaching his hand forward, Bjorn offered, "If you'll have me and Scratch is the person you have trusted all this time, I need to trust him too."

The captain shook hands with him and said, "See you in the morning unless you want to spend you last night on land. Scratch'll show you which rope bed is yours if you want to sleep on board.

"If you don't mind, I'll do that. That's the kind of bed I've always slept in. I'm not familiar with this city. Far too big for me. Might get lost if I wander about. I'll see what food is available and then I'll make my way aboard. Do I report to Scratch?"

"Ask for him if he's not at the top of the ladder when you board her. Tell him you're his new swab. He'll show you to a bed near him so he can give you orders easier. One more thing. Buy some peppermint syrup. You'll find an apothecary just down the street. Doc will fix you up.

Don't know how sensitive your stomach is to a rocking boat and we do rock."

Pleased with the prospect of free passage and duties to occupy his time aboard the schooner, Bjorn ordered the Inn's fare for the evening. He recognized it as a stew of some sort but it had vegetables in it that he'd never eaten before. The bread that came with the stew was like Mor's and made him homesick.

Finished with the meal, Bjorn took out one of the precious pieces of paper he'd stashed in his carpet bag when he left and used his stub pencil to write home. He told them he'd be leaving in the morning on the Domino and would send a letter to them as soon as he landed in the New World. He folded the letter carefully and sealed it, using wax from the candle on his table. Paying the inn keeper for the postage to mail the letter and his meal, he left the inn to find Doc and get the syrup. "Hope I won't need it on the crossing," he muttered aloud.

Opening the wood slatted door to the apothecary, Bjorn walked to the counter where a man he presumed was Doc sat on a wooden stool.

"Need some peppermint syrup?" came from the voice behind the counter. Inquisitive, but guarded eyes stared at him.

"Are you Doc?"

"I am. Captain Nor send you?"

"He did. Never sailed before. Hope the ship motion doesn't affect me too much."

"Lucky you came when you did. Nor's a fair man and looks after his crew, much better than some of the others who captain schooners out of here. Going to work your passage?"

"*Ja*, I'll answer to someone named Scratch for the next few weeks until we reach the New World. Know anything about this fellow Scratch?"

"Only that he likes his tobacco. Might want to by a small bag and have it ready when the man runs out of his stash. What ya think?"

"Cost much?"

"Na, your whole bill will be twenty five cents for the syrup and the 'baccy."

"Done." Bjorn fished the coins out of his belt pocket and thanked Doc for his help.

Returning the same way he'd come to find the Doc's shop, Bjorn stood and gazed at the three-masted schooner now in full view. Hesitating a little as he stood a ways from the ship, he couldn't believe how small it was. Would it make it across the ocean? "I wonder how many crew members there are. Wonder what the freight will be. Passengers?" Walking forward and grabbing the ropes that held the stairway's connection to the ship, Bjorn gingerly made his way up and boarded.

Chapter 5

"Reason for boarding?" came from a person dressed in black clothes sitting on a coil of rope, hardly visible in the moonless night.

Bjorn's startled reaction drew a snicker from the seated person. Stepping towards the speaker, he said, "I'm Bjorn, just hired on as Scratch's swab. Can you tell me where I'll find him?"

"You're looking at him. Welcome aboard, I think. Ever been on a ship?"

"No, sir," was Bjorn's quick answer. He wondered what he had gotten himself into this time.

"Bet you haven't seen a black man before either. Got your peppermint syrup?"

"*Ja*, I saw Doc. Captain said I could sleep on board tonight," offered Bjorn, deciding to see what reaction that got from the person he'd have to answer to over the next few weeks.

"Always I get the green ones. Never the experienced. Such is my lot in life! Come along, Laddie. Let's see what I can find for you for a bed. Got your gear with or do you have to go get it?"

"All I own is with me," and he hefted a carpet bag that contained a change of clothes, another pair of shoes and his Bible. "Hope to work my way to the Territories in the New World. Get some of that free land that is offered. Decided not to encumber myself, not knowing what the travel arrangements would be."

"Follow me, Laddie. You'll sleep on deck with me unless there's a storm. If it storms, we'll be too busy to sleep. If it rains, we'll hunker down with the cook in his cabin below. Here," and he pointed to one of the swinging rope beds just under the structure that led up to where the captain steered the ship. "This one'll be yours. Stow your bag in this trunk under the bed. I bunk just over there," and Scratch left him to continue monitoring whoever else decided to come aboard.

"Thanks, Scratch. I try and do the best I can as you teach me," offered Bjorn to the retreating figure at least another head taller than himself.

"You better. I don't take well to shirkers," came from the rumbling voice of the massive shouldered person entrusted to the riggings that would make the sails fly.

Tired from the unloading of the barge, from finding a ship's passage, from interviewing, from his visit with Doc, his boarding, and meeting his overseer, Bjorn lay on his rope bed and heard nothing until Scratch shook him at first daylight.

"Up and at 'em, Laddie. Get some grub from Cook as quick as you can. Meet me back here. Need to start readying the sails for cast off. Use that bucket over there and throw its contents overboard," offered Scratch with a smile on his face.

Surprised that he'd slept so well in such a strange open area, Bjorn rose, looking for the bucket. Used to a rope bed from his childhood, he'd quickly adapted to the swaying of the schooner as it gently rocked in the harbor up against its docking.

Moving below deck and letting his nose lead the way to the galley, Bjorn gaped at the meal set out and ready for the crew. Flapjacks, bacon, fresh fruit, coffee, and some kind of mush. Guilt overcame him, knowing that none of his family ever had this much food available for any meal and certainly not at breakfast. Not knowing how hard he'd have to work, when the next meal would be or what it might be, Bjorn took a generous portion of all offered, ate as quickly as he could and made his way back to where he'd agreed to meet Scratch.

Bucket and mop in hand, Scratch came around the foremast bulkhead. "Here. Get the grime off the deck. Can't afford to slip on any spills. Soon time to hoist sail."

Bjorn completed his task of swabbing all the decks and then he heard a "Cast off" that came from Captain Nor above in the crows' nest. Least that's what Scratch had called the wood structure they'd slept under. He'd heard of a crows' nest before in the Nordic stories of the Viking sailors. Vikings carried crows or ravens in a cage at the top of a mast. When visibility was poor, the early sailors released a bird and followed its flight course. They knew that a bird always flew towards the closest land. Did Captain Nor have a bird cage too?

Bjorn watched the men ready sails and stayed out of the way, mesmerized by the efficiency of the crew and the mechanical way that each man did what was expected without direction. Under Scratch's leadership, ten hands took their positions, each alongside a pile of rope, and pulled. Sails rose to half-mast as the ship made its way out of the harbor. Where had the crew come from? Seemed to Bjorn that there was someone from every nationality. The strength of the men was evident in their broad shoulders and muscular legs. The amazing thing was that little was spoken; tasks were accomplished with little direction from Scratch.

Clearing the harbor, the crew set the sails at full mast, tied off the roping and effortlessly moved on to their other duties. "How lucky I am to have signed on with this crew," thought Bjorn. "I may live to see the New World after all."

"Learn anything?" came from that same rumbling voice of the night before.

"To stay out of the way when I don't know what to do," retorted Bjorn with a lilt in his voice.

"Glad you did. Glad you also had sense to stand around and watch. Won't be long and one of those ropes will be your responsibility."

"How often do the sails come down?"

Scratch did just that, scratched the hairs on his muscular chest. "You are green. We sail at full mast as much as we can unless the wind's strength dictates otherwise."

"What do you need me to do?" queried Bjorn.

"Go down and help Cook until I get orders from Captain Nor. Not sure if we are stopping anywhere else or if we are heading for open seas."

Turning to take the stairs leading below, Bjorn found most of what he thought must be the crew eating breakfast. Stepping into the galley, he rolled up the sleeves of his shirt and began to wash the dishes that had accumulated from the fixing of the meal. Cook continued to make flapjacks and fry bacon until those present were satisfied. He grabbed two covered platters, filled each with a sampling from the available food and said, "Thanks for stepping in, washing some of the ever-present stack of dirty dishes. Take these two to Captain and Scratch. You'll find them in the crows' nest, setting the quadrants for the trip."

Hands now full, Bjorn wondered how he was to get up the rope ladders with the food, not spill them and yet keep his balance. He found that rope ladder reaching almost straight up. He leaned into the ladder as he maneuvered each step up. He was able to balance his body, make progress up and not spill the contents. Once at the top, Bjorn set the two platters on the small deck, got himself the rest of the way up, picked up the trays again and took them to the doorway of the Captain's quarters. "Here, sirs. Complements of Cook," offered Bjorn.

"You brought them? How'd you manage not to dump either or both coming up the ladder?" asked Scratch with a tinge of disbelief in his voice.

"Leaned in with my body. Worked today but I'm not sure it'd work if the wind were howling and the ship was rocking," stated Bjorn with a little pride in his voice.

"Used to work, aren't you, Laddie," came from Scratch between mouthfuls of food.

"Used to doing what needs to be done – whatever that might be. Used to hard work, long days, and little time for me."

"What did you say you did up in that Nordic area?" Captain questioned.

"Sheep herded mostly. The just weaned lambs were my charge. Had help from Shep and Beck."

"Shep? Beck? Brothers?" asked the captain.

With laughter in his voice, Bjorn answered, "*Nei*, better than that. Two sheep dogs that took orders without question. Rest of the time I was behind a horse and plow."

Finishing their meal, the two gathered their utensils and handed the pile to Bjorn. "Careful on the way down. It's trickier than you'd think. See what you can do for Cook. He's not had help in a long time. When I'm done here, I'll call for you and begin teaching you rope knots and names of the sails," offered Scratch as he closed the door behind Bjorn on his way out.

Chapter 6

"Storm coming!" woke Bjorn and he found himself dumped out of bed. "Secure everything loose like I've been teaching you. Going below to wake the rest of the crew."

Fear crept through Bjorn's body looking in the direction Scratch had pointed. He saw nothing and wondered if it were a dream. Shuffling came from below deck. Assembling as they did to hoist sail to leave port, each stood by for direction to lower sails. With commands from Scratch, the larger sails came down, their ropes were tied off and secured. As efficiently, Bjorn stowed anything that was "not tied down" like Scratch had taught him. Going below, he began to help Cook who was busy stoking the fire and securing the loose items he'd had out preparing food. Bjorn washed and scrubbed pots and pans quickly. Just as efficiently Cook stashed each item behind doors that had latches. As they finished stowing most of the cooking pots, pans, and serving dishes, the ship began to roll side to side and then buck forward and aft. "Guess I'm going to find out if I'll need my syrup," stated Bjorn. He didn't have time to ponder more, for he heard his summons to come above deck, loud and clear.

"Bjorn! Laddie! Bjorn!" yelled Scratch.

Struggling to climb the steps and reaching the main deck, Bjorn hung on to anything available as he made his way over to Scratch.

"Need you, Laddie. Lift these ropes. One's tangled around my ankle. Careful. Deck's slippery. One misstep and you're overboard."

Bjorn put his back to the deck's wall, felt secured and lifted the coiled rope. "Clear" came from Scratch, and Bjorn dropped the coiling. The dropping threw his body off balance and he found himself sliding on the deck as the ship bucked a wave. Away now from the protection of the wall, he reached out in front of him and along the sides as he slid, hoping to grab something to stop his inevitable pitch into the roiling sea. Darkness did not help. The edge of the main deck loomed in front of him. One more pitch and he'd be overboard. Steel hands grabbed his pants suspenders. The elastic tightened on his chest. He felt himself snapping back and thrown into a cubby filled with unused sail. "Green!" was uttered as the person moved away. Who it was or why that person was about and able to save him Bjorn never did find out, but he now knew what the statement meant – a life for a life. He'd helped Scratch and somebody had saved him from a watery grave.

True to Scratch's promise that they'd sleep below when it rained, Bjorn slept when he could on one of the benches in the galley. He kept the peppermint syrup handy in his back pocket. Surprisingly, his stomach did not get upset. Most likely his being used to uneven ground and maneuvering across it on the mountainside at a rapid pace to keep a lamb from harm had conditioned his body for sailing as well. The storm raged! At times he wondered if the schooner would split apart as it cracked and moaned from the wind's strength. At other times he imagined it flooded and sinking. Any sleep that came included nightmares, hinged on some kind of survival connected to the water and wind.

Dawn came with the seas calming as the winds abated. Cook woke him this time, handing him a cup of strong coffee. "Better see what Scratch needs. Don't suppose you'll have to scrub the decks but never know. Storm seems about over." Bjorn drank quickly, but didn't take time to eat, unsure how food would settle in his stomach but not willing to trust luck.

Sails and rigging were strewn across the deck. Crew members were busy sorting sail, splicing rope, and checking the masts for splints and cracks.

Scratch called to him; "Get Captain coffee. Be sure it's strong! He'll want more than one cup. Move!"

Move he did. Down below. Found a clean syrup pail, filled it with hot coffee, put the lid on it and raced as fast as he could up the stairs leading to the main deck. Sail and rope lay scattered across the deck. Navigating the rope ladder, he was careful so that the pail with hot coffee didn't touch his skin. Captain's cabin was equally strewn with ship's log papers, maps, spy glasses, clothing, and trinkets. Bjorn opened the lid of the pail, took the cup he'd brought, and poured the coffee. Reaching in his pocket, he offered his precious vial of peppermint syrup. "Need a sweetener, Captain?"

"Sweetener would be good, not for my stomach but for my soul." Captain rubbed his back, trying to relieve some of the tension of the night. "Stack paper here," gestured the tired man. "Any trinkets back in this drawer. Maps go over here on this shelf by the window. Anything you're not sure of put on my desk and I'll sort it later. Who sent you?"

"Cook," was the reply as Bjorn began the task of making order out of chaos.

"Heard you almost were food for the fish?"

"*Ja*, someone grabbed these suspenders as I was about to take a bath."

"Know who?"

"Nei, wish I did. All I heard as I was thrown on the pile of spare sail in that cubby on deck was, 'Green'!"

"May be green but I understand you do know how to work. If you want to make more *penger* as you call it, I'd be glad to hire you for another trip or two."

"Let me think about it. Need to get to port first, see how overwhelming it is for someone like me who has hardly been away from that secluded mountainside where I was born." Bjorn busied himself with the clean-up for a while and then asked, "Once we reach the New World, how many days before you set sail for Trondheimsfjorden again?" queried Bjorn, continuing to sort the floor's new paper rug decorated with a trinket here and there.

"Two days."

"That should give me enough time to find a group that is going over the mountains to the Territories. I need to see what joining with them means. How costly it will be. If I can work my way as I did with you."

"And if you can't find a group?" asked the captain.

"One way or another I'll let you know in enough time to find a replacement for me if I decide to make my way over the trails by wagon and carts to that area where land is free for the taking."

Chapter 7

Days and nights blended into one as time passed on the fairly calm open sea. The schooner sped across the water under full sail. Though he asked, no one admitted to saving him from the plunge into the wild stormy sea. Nightmares still haunted his sleep. Bjorn would wake in a cold sweat. Such times found him rising and sitting on the same coil of rope that Scratch sat on when Bjorn first boarded the vessel. Those were the nights that found him going down in the galley in the early morning hours and helping Cook with the crew's breakfast.

"Port must be getting closer," Bjorn thought. Less fruits for breakfast now. Bacon was beginning to taste rancid. Mold had to be scraped off the cheese rounds as each was unsealed from its cloth wrappings. Vegetables for the fish chowders weren't as plentiful either. Cook's energy seemed resilient. When a small disruption rocked his daily routine, he met it with a feistiness few people could muster considering the closeness of the limited kitchen quarters and its options.

And then it happened! "Land ho!" came from the crows' nest.

Bjorn scrambled quickly to the foredeck as most of the crew did, anxious to see that first sighting for himself. Awe overcame him. The massiveness of the harbor sent an uneasiness about him when the schooner sailed into port. He was glad for the captain's offer to rehire him should he choose not to continue his dream. Could he find a group that was going where he wanted to go? Would he be able to work his way?

"Bjorn. Bjorn."

Hearing his name, he realized he may be helping with the sails for the last time. He hurried up on deck, took his position on the rope for the smaller sail and waited for Scratch's orders to manage his sail.

Docked. How effortless it had happened. Bjorn went to his bed and gathered all his belongings into his carpet bag. Deciding to leave the bag on board the schooner while he sought a group, Bjorn went to ask permission to do so. Climbing the rope stairs to the Captain's quarters came so much easier now.

"Bjorn, you leaving us? Thought any about staying with us for the year?" came from the captain.

"Not sure yet what I will do. Promise to come back and tell you my decision. Wondered if I could leave my bag here with you?"

"Sure."

" Any idea where I might find a group going where I want to go?" asked Bjorn.

"Not really. Sorry. Best advice I can give you is to listen to the people talking. If you hear your Norsk spoken, those are the people I would inquire of and trust. Glad you're leaving your bag here. Lots of riff raff out there. Steal you blind."

Bjorn shook Captain's hand, made his way down the stairs, found Scratch and did the same. From his pocket, Bjorn removed the 'baccy he's bought at the apothecary.

"Thanks, Laddie. Had my last smoke last night, knowing we'd be in port today. Means I won't have to fight the rest of the crew looking to replace their stash too. I can wait until later this evening to do so."

"Where's the closest apothecary? Need to replace my peppermint syrup. Lacing your coffees the morning after the storm at sea almost emptied my bottle," offered Bjorn with a smile on his face.

"Just up Harbor Avenue on the right, the same road you'll walk to find someone heading west to the new frontier," answered Scratch, pointing as best he could while he was fixing his pipe for a smoke. Once again, goodbyes were said and Bjorn was on his way.

Walking the ropes that led from schooner to deck was much easier now than when he had boarded. Time at sea taught him lots and conditioned his body, giving him muscular strength he'd never had. As he got off the rope gangplank onto the dock, Bjorn wobbled a bit, surprised he had what some called "sea legs." Once he stood to the side and established his balance, he began his search for someone speaking like those he left back at the *gard*.

"Apothecary. Where was it?" thought Bjorn as he left the schooner and looked up the street. "Better replace that syrup when I can. Never know what I'll have to eat from now on and when I'll find food." Seeing a weather-worn sign with a mortar and pestle on it hanging from a rooftop, Bjorn headed up the sloping hill towards it. Scratch was right. The small shop was crowded with all sorts of people replacing or getting a supply of medications and necessities. Travelers, ship's crew, locals, and more. Bjorn waited for most to complete their purchases before he approached the "Doc" behind this shop's counter.

"Need?" was all that came from the Oriental featured man who had both hands on the smoothened plank that served as a worktop.

"Peppermint syrup, please."

"Vial or pint?"

"Better make it a pint. Not sure when I'll find another apothecary."

This doc reached under his counter and produced a brown colored bottle with the shop's affixed hand written label, "Peppermint Syrup." Paying for his purchase, Bjorn headed back up the street, looking for a group that was dressed like his folks back home.

Checking the people in the groups was like looking for more of the same fish in the same pond. The clothing some men wore looked like crew from the ships at port. Others wore what he was wearing – beeches, hand-made linen shirts tucked in and belted, hose secured by the bottom of the breeches and heavy serviceable leather shoes of some sort. So similar was each man's appearance that he began to look for women with blonde hair and wearing the clothes he'd seen worn by the traveling women on the streets of Trondheim. He spotted a group a ways ahead whose two women had bonnets with unruly blonde hair, freed during haste to disembark.

Jostling people as he went, Bjorn hurried forward, always keeping an eye on the women. Once behind the two families, he listened as the captain had instructed. Their words weren't just as he had learned Norsk but similar. Bjorn decided they were from a different region. Didn't matter. What could he lose? When they stopped at the top of the rise where streets met to continue on or go left and right, Bjorn stepped ahead to face one of the elderly gentlemen. "*Unnskyld meg* (excuse me)." And then he continued, "*Va eb ak leste* – Going out west?"

Startled that someone would speak to them in their language, the group of six chattered to the other at once and kept their eyes on Bjorn. "*Ja, ve* are," came from the fellow who seemed to be the eldest of the three men in the group. Haltingly, he answered, "Are you?"

"I hope to get to the Territories north of Carter's Cove. I'm looking for a group that's going in that direction and want to join with them. I'm willing to work for my inclusion in the group. Whatever way I can," offered Bjorn, hoping he was speaking slowly enough so that they would understand. He was so used to speaking the English of the crew that he forgot to speak Norsk to this group in front of him.

"We're joining a wagon – ah – ah – train in the morning." The man hesitated a bit trying to remember the English, thinking for the words to use. Seeing the other man nod his head, the first continued. "You are welcome to come with us. Talk to the – wagon – ah – master. See if he has place for you." Extending his hand, he continued, "Leif Larson. He's Helmer Bergen. Son, Rolf." The three women who stood behind the men listening intently were not included in the introduction of names.

"I'm Bjorn Hanson. Where are you staying? Where can I meet you in the morning?"

"We stay at the Wayfarer Inn. Yust up the street, I tink. Meet at daylight. Want to start early. Get ourselves organized. Wagon master's scout comes. Lead us to the train." Offering his hand to shake, Bjorn did so, shaking hands with the other two and returned back to the deck and gangplank where the schooner was docked, satisfied that he was on his way to the Territories and the fulfillment of his dream. The cold pattering of raindrops didn't dampen his spirits.

Chapter 8

Bjorn found that dreaming was easy. Fulfilling the wishes was another story. Once he was back on the schooner, he spent time writing home. He told them of his ability to work for his passage, that he'd found other Nordic people going to the Territories and would join with them if the wagon master would let him.

Sleep eluded him most of the night. Rising early and with a little sadness in his voice, Bjorn found the two men that had been so kind to him as he left the Old Country bound for the New World and his dream. He said his goodbyes to Captain Nor and Scratch, thanking both for their patience and understanding for his lack of sailing skills when he boarded the schooner. Over the last five weeks since leaving the *gard*, the schooner became home, comfort in a world filled with uncertainty at this point in his life.

Reaching the rope ladder that connected the schooner with to the dock, he heard a voice high in the rigging of the one mast; "Good luck, greenie." Startled, Bjorn turned, lifted his head high while shielding his eyes from the bright sun, waved and pounded his heart as he did so – a signal he hoped would mean thankfulness to the man above – knowing full well that this person was the one who'd saved him from being "lost" at sea.

Few were about in this early morning hour. The usual merchants, their wares in baskets on their shoulders or on their heads, shouted the sale of their contents from fish to vegetables to cheese to cloth or whatever else could easily be carried. Bjorn chose a fresh bread loaf and paid the coins. He did the same for a small cheese wedge and tucked both into his carpet bag, not knowing where he'd find his next meal.

The Inn sign waved in the wind that blew gently off the port water as daylight broke over the horizon. Bjorn sighed with relief and headed in the direction of it and its mud filled hitching post where horses stood. Families were up and about, beginning to collect their belongings and secure them in a horse or oxen driven cart, hired for this purpose.

"*Got Morgen*" (good morning), offered Bjorn as he approached Leif and Helmer busy loading. "The rains have passed through. Makes packing easier."

"*Ja*. Seems like we got more now than when we first left the Old Country," muttered Helmer as he put the last cover on a barrel stuffed to brimming over.

"All you got?" came from Leif with amazement in his voice, pointing to the carpet bag in Bjorn's left hand.

"*Ja*, didn't know how I was going to get from one place to the next or where I'd be," offered Bjorn with a smile evident in his voice.

"Wish the womenfolk thought the same way. Told them we'd probably leave most of what we brought by the side of the trail. Make the cart lighter up the mountain. Didn't want to listen. We'll see . . ." and Helmer stopped talking as another man approached.

"Larson? Bergen?" came from this new person.

"*Ja*," both answered.

"And you?" questioned the dark skinned individual dressed in leather breeches and a shirt. It was obvious he was looking for someone who had just disembarked one of the ships, now moored in the harbor.

Extending his hand in greeting, he said, "I'm Bjorn Hanson. And you?"

"Delaware," was the answer as he gripped Bjorn's hand hard. "I'm the scout if you're the families that are traveling west over the mountains."

"We are. Glad you came. Need a guide to find our way out," answered Leif in his halting English as he stepped up to shake hands. "This is Helmer. Rest of our families will be here shortly."

"Who do I ask if there is room for me to join the train? I'm willing to do whatever I can to earn my passage," said Bjorn with a little trepidation in his voice.

"Know anything about horses?" queried Delaware, skeptical of the capabilities of the young man facing him.

"Do. I spent half my time in the Old Country on the mountainside herding stubborn yearling lambs. Rest was spent behind a drag or plowshare harnessed to a draft horse or two unless the King needed men to fight his wars."

"You'll do. Always room for fresh hands who have some sense of rugged life. Won't be an easy trip over those passes. Trails are rough, often changing from the landslides."

"Will the women be safe?" spoke Helmer with concern in his voice.

"If you mean from Indians like me, that's why I'm along. Our tribe is friendly. So are most of the rest if they're treated right. Need to leave. Get the rest," came like an order delivered to the Leif and Helmer. "Anyone not here by the time I get back from the apothecary gets left," and he turned, making his way across the street.

Both men scrambled towards the Inn, realizing this scout had little patience and meant what he said about leaving.

Without reluctance, Helmer handed the reins of the lead cart's horse to Delaware and seated himself on a barrel. His son and wife settled just behind on a wood carved trunk. Leif sat ready in the other cart. His wife and daughter found place to sit amid all the belongings.

"Ride Wing," gestured Delaware and he watched, genuinely surprised as Bjorn mounted the saddleless animal with ease. "Keep close together. The streets out to where the train is gathering are narrow." Following instructions, the small group slowly made their way to the edge of town.

Chapter 9

Delaware moved his new charges quickly but cautiously through the shops and living quarters that made up this large community. Wheeled and pedestrian traffic collided at many intersections, making it difficult for units like the two families with their herded animals to stay together. Once outside the edges of the city proper, the congestion of people and animals lessened and Rolf's five prized cows heavy with calves responded to his directions quicker. Reaching the others already gathered, Bjorn was amazed at the forty or so wagons already circled. Delaware's group was the last to arrive, and he issued instructions. "Water the horses and livestock. Take care of your necessities. Train leaves at noon."

Bjorn dismounted and handed Wing's reins to Delaware. "Trained him well. Thanks for letting me ride him."

"Come. Meet Stone. He's as the name indicates, hard as nails to get along with, firm on his expectations but so capable in any crisis," explained the scout. "I've been with him for five years. Can't find a fairer man. Demands respect and gets it. Let's see if he has a spare horse for you to ride."

By the demeanor of Stone, Bjorn was sure that he was capable. Hair bristled from under the stocking cap. Leather shirt and leggings form fit his muscular body. Delaware made the introduction and indicated his feelings for allowing Bjorn to join the group.

"How far you headed?" came from the steel-voiced mountain man in front of him.

"To Carter's Cove and then North into the Territories. I hope to see if I can find land in the Old Crossing area on the Red River," returned Bjorn as he kept eye contact with the man who could make his journey easier.

"Know anything about animals?"

"Mounted Wing, unsaddled. Handled him well," offered Delaware.

"Spent most of my life herding sheep in the Nordic mountains. Spent some time behind work horses and a drag, harrowing ground," answered Bjorn in clipped sentences, realizing this wagon master wanted simple information and not a life story.

"Take that sorrel over there tied to the cook's wagon. She's yours for the trip out west. You can help scout. You'll get your instructions and assignments from Delaware. Take good care of Red. Gather your belongings and secure them to her. Put the carpet bag in the cook's wagon. Train will leave at noon." Looking at Delaware, he said, "The number is fifty." Leaning down to Bjorn, he continued, "Listen to him and don't disappoint me," cautioned Stone as he extended his hand to seal the bargain and quickly rode off to talk to the wagon masters gathering in a group at the river's edge.

Bjorn found himself aboard another horse, with a bed roll behind, and a water jar tied at his knee. He waited patiently for direction, grateful for the opportunity to work his way to the New World.

"Follow me," came from Delaware and they headed down the well-worn oxen and wagon cart trail, away from the wagons and the rush of the large city behind them.

Scout? What did that mean? Shoot whatever moved for food? Look for berries and vegetables suitable to eat? Bjorn didn't think it would be looking for Indians. Delaware was one of them. Were there poachers like those in the Nordic mountains who'd steal animals from the trains? Take from the small herds of cows, sheep, chickens or a pig or two? Delaware signaled him to ride beside him, and Bjorn moved Red up next to Wind.

"Need to get to Fort Frederick," began Delaware, "before the train does. A stone house is built over a spring. Couple lives there. The wife prepares a hot meal for everyone. She needs to know how many are in the train so she knows how much stew to fix. Her cooking the first meal gives the women a chance to get accustomed to traveling by wagon. Helps make food preparation easier the first day of the journey. Families won't need to use their provisions, especially if they are greenies who have never made meals over open fires. Time enough for that in the morning once camp has been established."

"Greenie." There was that word again. "At least this time it isn't directed at me," Bjorn mumbled to himself. Still unsure of his role with the train, he decided to ask Delaware, "You know I'm willing. I'm not sure how able I am. What I don't know, I hope you'll teach me quickly. I learn fast."

Delaware nodded his consent. "Fort Frederick borders on the Potomac River. Train follows the river out of here to the fort. The Chesapeake and Ohio Rivers pass through the same area. The spot where these two rivers cross is where many wagon trains camp their first night. Stone won't want the members of our train to mingle very much with the others. The less confrontation with other train members early on makes better following of Stone's rules. Never know when you have a poacher whose interest is to scout our group and come later to steal whatever seems valuable. First task for you is to make sure that our people don't go visiting."

The two kept a steady pace, stopping at noon to water the horses. From the pouch hanging from the trappings of his horse, Delaware extracted *pemmican* and jerky. "Ever eaten anything like this?" he asked as he handed Bjorn a small round cake.

"Don't think so. What is it?" asked Bjorn as he took the piece of each that was offered and waited for an explanation.

"My people make the *pemmican* in your left hand from dried strips of meat pounded into paste. Fat and berries are mixed into the paste and pressed into little cakes like that. The other, jerky, is dried meat."

"*Ja*, we dry meat too. I've had jerky many times up in the mountainside alone as I tended sheep."

"You know then to chew slowly. Both tend to expand and absorb moisture once you chew. Water jar full?"

"*Ja*," stated Bjorn. "I'm green but not that green," came from him with a little smile in the voice.

"Water is available here so drink as much as you need. It'll take a bit to get used to *pemmican*. We carry it so we don't have to stop, kill something and cook. Especially when we need to keep our whereabouts hidden. Helps keep our scalps," was Delaware's comment with a smile in his voice.

Riding through a small village made Bjorn aware of what life was like in the backcountry of the New World. Sometimes at a rundown shack along the trail they stop and share a hot, tasty meal from the pot over the outside cooking fire. At other places small hamlets existed. Each village usually offered a stables, blacksmith shop, mercantile store, a granary, one or two inns for people to sleep and sometimes an apothecary or someone who cared for the sick. Seeing a sign where he thought he might find items needed for his journey, Bjorn offered, "Don't have many provisions. Should we stop here so I can get supplies you think I might need along the way?"

"Got an extra shirt, pants, shoes and two pair of socks?"

"*Ja*."

"That's about all you need. Stone furnishes food and fire arms. We'll be expected to do some hunting and fishing. Can you shoot?"

"*Ja*, had to learn to keep the wolves away from the sheep. Handle a slingshot pretty good too. Less noise in the mountains. Brought mine with," answered Bjorn as he patted his saddlebag where it was stashed. "Don't have any smooth pebbles but the rivers and trails should have what I need."

"Delaware," came from a stocky man standing just outside the blacksmith shop as the two rode through this small village. "When's the train coming?"

"Shouldn't be too far behind us, Blackie. This bunch seems better prepared than the last. Didn't see too much work for you," was Delaware's response as he stopped briefly in front of the man.

"Hope there is some work. Could use a few coins."

"Never know. What I saw might surprise me. Their wood carts appear built better than the ones closer to Carter's Cove. Should withstand the trail better. See you on the road back in about three months," and he wheeled his horse on down the trail with Bjorn following.

The carved out road with three separate sets of ruts from oxen, carts and wagons wound its way across ridges and in that way avoided swampland as much as possible. "Green," thought Bjorn. Not the same green as he'd been called but the color green. Lush meadows with waist-high grass waving in the wind amazed Bjorn. Never had he seen grazing land such as this. The gentle rolling hills gave him hope that he'd be able to have a *gard* of his own, a farm plot big enough to support his family and earn enough *penger* to afford their tickets to come.

"Not far now. Over the next rise. You'll see the stone house off in the distance along the river. We'll need to ford the Chesapeake to reach it.

"River fast flowing?" asked Bjorn, used to the rush of the mountain's rivers back home.

Need to find the best place to cross. Some of those wagon masters haven't driven a wagon or oxcart, let alone forded a river. We'll need to help where we can. I'll ride ahead and tell Marta to plan on fifty tonight. Shouldn't be a problem. She's got a big cast iron pot that she hangs over the fire pit. See the hut, Bjorn?"

"*Ja.*"

"See those two trees down by the river? The two that look like a y?"

Bjorn nodded and asked, "I go there and wait?"

"Not just wait. See what the crossing looks like. How wide? How fast the water's flowing? Is the other side easy to access? If your sheep could cross it, the wagon train can. Take Red across and back. She's used to fording water. If she seems nervous in any way as you first cross, back out and try another spot. Horses sense more than we realize." With a gentle nudging in Wind's quarters, Delaware was off to alert Marta that the train was coming.

Bjorn rode ahead to the trees along the river, dismounted when he got there and allowed Red to drink. Flow didn't seem overly fast. Water depth looked to be a foot or two from what he could see. Satisfied, he remounted and urged Red across. Letting the horse set the pace, Bjorn slackened the reins and let her choose the path. That she had crossed many rivers and probably this very spot more than once was evident in the ease in her movement through the water and up the bank on the other side.   Bjorn took the time to ride up and down the riverbank's edge on this far side to see if there were an easier spot to ford. Finding none, he guided Red back to where they had first come across and made the return trip.

Dismounting on the other side near a clump of grass under a ways from the bank, Bjorn tied his horse, took off his stocking cap and scratched his head. Sweaty from the ride and the challenges that the early morning had been, Bjorn took off his shirt, pants, socks and boots and waded into the stream for a quick bath before the train arrived. The cool water made him shiver as he scrubbed as best he could with a little sand in his hand. Satisfied that he taken at least one layer of dirt off, he returned to the bank and sat on a downed log to wind dry. Spotting Delaware returning, he redressed and waited, wondering how this first fording would go.

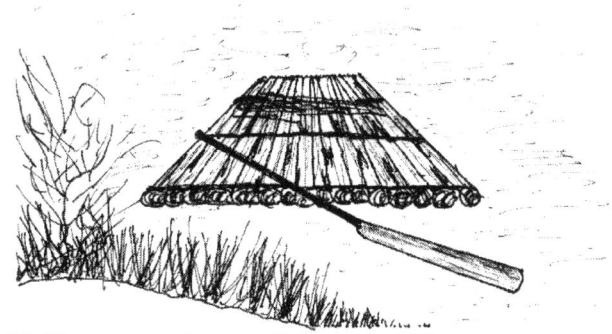

"Will we need to build a skow?"

"Skow? I don't know. What is it?" came from Bjorn with a quizzical look to his face.

"It's a light raft that has beams. Each wagon is unloaded and the barrels and wood boxes floated across. The empty wagon would be driven or pulled across."

"Nei, the river's not that deep. How is it made?"

With patience in his voice, Delaware instructed, "We'd need to take those fallen trees over there, roots and all, and rope them together."

"So we'd be building a skow now before they come if it's needed?

"Would. A few of those people who have the big wagons will have to unload and see that their belongings are split in loads for two crossings. Some of these same folks have really heavy wagons. The wheels may sink in the river sand so we need to be cautious. Those heavily loaded wagons will have to be last to cross so that the riverbed stays firm as possible for the rest who cross first. Stone's been riding up and down the line of wagons and carts as they've moved along the trail to here, deciding the order of crossing."

"Those are the same people who will be leaving part of what they brought along the trail, right?" decided Bjorn.

"*Ja*, as you say" mimicked Delaware of the way Bjorn said yes, "but to tell them that now would cause many tears with the women so we let them learn the hard way."

"Are all these wagons going to Carter's Cove?" questioned Bjorn as Delaware dismounted.

"Not sure. Haven't had time to ask Stone. The rivers meet here. Some may wait for another train that is going south. Some may leave us when we get to Port Canton or Lake Erie. Doesn't matter what each chooses. Others join along the way. Fifty is about the limit of people Stone will take. Too big a group makes them string out too far and might mean more breakdowns along the way."

Bjorn went over to Red and checked the hoofs for pebbles. "She's a good mount."

"Stone must trust your judgment. Few have been given the privilege of riding her west. Sleep when you can. We'll hear the rumbling of the wheels long before we'll see them. Have another piece?" asked Delaware as he reached in his leather pouch and handed Bjorn another hunk of jerky. "It'll be a while before we get any of that stew she's cooking. Smelled good too."

Chapter 10

"Thunder? Didn't look like rain when I decided to nap," thought Bjorn, awakening just as the sun was at four o'clock according to his estimate. "Has to be the wagons," came through his mind, remembering someone telling him of the noise they make when the whole group gets moving. Animals braying. People yelling at their oxen and horses. Wooden wheels moving over uneven ground. He jumped when Delaware approached from behind, not hearing the Indian's soft movement. Turning to face him, Bjorn asked, "Want me to do anything?"

"Rode out and talked briefly to Stone. Says this group is pretty good to obey orders. We'll see. This is the first time we ford water. Need to keep them in order like Stone has lined them up. Mount up. You may have to help guide an ox or two into the water. Stubborn animals. Don't like to get wet."

"Silvis is first, I see. That small cart and ox look like it won't make it over the mountain," commented Bjorn. "Are oxcarts meant for mountain climbing? Ox is a young one. If the cart holds together, the ox will make it."

"You'll be surprised which will give us trouble and which will survive," added Delaware as he stationed himself to the right of where the carts and wagons were to enter the river. "Silvis offered to unload his cart and be the ferry for those on foot if we need more than the scow."

Bjorn mounted Red and guided him to the river's edge to the left of where the train was to enter and stationed himself there as a guide for the best place to cross.

"How deep is it?" came from the stout, bearded fellow called Silvis as he got off his seat on the smallest of carts.

"No more than knee high if you head for that tree over there, Silvis," assured Bjorn, pointing to the other side. "Ox give you trouble in water?"

"She'll do fine," he remarked and waded in to walk the animal and cart over to the other side.

As Silvis got his ox and cart half way across, Delaware told the next rig in line to enter the water and follow. Bjorn watched, amazed at how smoothly the crossing was going, each respectful of the other and helpful once on the other side. Suddenly, one of the heavily loaded wagons pulled by two sturdy horses broke rank and came quickly towards Bjorn. Just as suddenly, Stone came from behind, made for the bank and yelled, "Back in line, Hiram. Wait your turn." Those who had decided to follow Hiram heard the harsh, demanding voice of the Stone and stopped, easing themselves back in line when space became available.

"*Nei*, we'll start another group crossing – those who have horses can manage," spouted the determined Hiram, impatient to wait, so sure he was of himself and his team's ability.

Bjorn turned and yelled, "Back in line!" signaling for him to stop. Team and heavily loaded wagon had too much momentum going and couldn't have stopped. Hiram, his horses and wagon charged over the bank, oblivious to the directions, and began their crossing. One third of the way over, the team faltered and so did the wagon. Both encountered a deep pooling area where the water swirled, causing chutes capable of drowning animals and man caught in its undertow, before the river water moved downstream. Stumbling horses triggered the wagon to tip sideways, spilling its contents into the water. Hiram flew the opposite direction head first into the stream and closer to the river's bank.

Bjorn, used to swimming in frigid, fast moving streams, dismounted and splashed his way over to the floating face down body, yanked on the red suspenders and lifted. The strength he'd gleaned from working the ropes on the schooner enabled Bjorn to raise Hiram up enough so he could steady himself in the water's torrent. Seeing Delaware's signal to return to the side of the river where he'd been guiding the crossings, Bjorn left Hiram, his team and his wagon with its contents floating downriver.

Stone said nothing to the shocked Hiram when he entered the river and headed to the overturned cart still harnessed to the two bays struggling to find footing in the swirling water. Stone cut the horses' reins, freeing them from the weight of the wagon. They lumbered their way across the river to the other side. Once up on the bank, already forded cart drivers took the remains of their harness ropes and tied them to a nearby tree. Hiram stood in the water by his wagon, unsure what to do. One of the oxcart drivers took three ropes out to Hiram and helped him attach each to the axel and rung. The ropes were dragged back through the water where a pair of draft horses stood ready to pull the wagon free. Once righted, the wagon came through the water to the other edge, sometimes floating, sometimes on its own wheels. Few helped Hiram retrieve the wagon's contents. He became an example for all who did not obey orders.

Those who chose to unload their carts or wagons waited until all had crossed and then took turns using the skows made earlier by Bjorn and Delaware. The few animals that were unwilling to ford the water were corralled on the skows too. Bjorn watched the process as horses, mules and oxen made trips across and back. The reloading of each wagon or cart made him realize how time consuming other crossings of other wider and faster flowing rivers would be. "Won't get far on those days.

Stone's a good man, demanding but smart. I'm glad to be a part of this train," reflected Bjorn. "Wonder if I'll ever reach Old Crossing in the Northwest Territories."

Chapter 11

Camp quieted as dark descended on the caravan. The few sheep, cows, chickens, horses, and oxen roamed free within the make-shift fence of the wagons now circled wheel to wheel with their rungs facing out. Weary travelers came to the huge kettle supported over the fire pit by an iron shaped tripod that held it in place. Bodies were tired from the stress of a new experience and for some their first fording of a river. Ladle in hand, Marta filled each bowl with a wonderful smelling stew. Her oldest daughter passed out slices of fresh bread. A pot of strong coffee sat on the edge of the fire, keeping warm. Last to eat were Stone, Delaware and Bjorn, returning from their scouting the areas and making sure that all were circled-up.

"*Takk* (thanks)," uttered Bjorn as he took the food handed to him, weary from the *learning as you go* expectations both Delaware and Stone used to teach him how to scout.

"*Velkommen* (you're welcome)," whispered the daughter in a sweet, shy voice, keeping her head down all the while. With a smile on his face but too tired to enquire why she could speak his language, Bjorn moved over to where Delaware and Stone were seated.

"That's why I went to tell Marta the number to cook for and didn't send you," teased Delaware, seeing the grin on Bjorn's tired face.

"*Ja*, I probably wouldn't have come back as soon as you did. A man gets hungry for hearing his native tongue spoken, especially when it comes from such a sweet sounding voice."

"Could settle down here. Land's available," stated Stone in his usual flat, hard voice.

"Nei, I need to go north and see if I can find my Uncle Olaf, Mor's brother. I'm too young to settle down yet, too green." There was that word again – green. Bjorn knew he was just that, inexperienced but grateful for his fortune to learn from people like Scratch and now Delaware. Hiram learned why it is important to follow orders, having lost most of his belongings when the wagon overturned. Bjorn knew there'd be more hard lessons along the way. His hope was that he was strong enough to survive the wild country that he'd travel."

"You take first watch, Bjorn. Walk the perimeter of the train outside and inside. Keep an eye for anyone who wanders over to the other trains. Don't want any mixing tonight. Too hard to keep track of everyone. Don't want any poachers to know who's worth stealing from in this group."

"And if I see someone wandering?"

"Delaware, get him that gun in the cook's wagon. You can shoot one?"

"*Ja.*"

"These first few nights, sleep is not something I'll get to do," declared Stone. "I'll be scouting the area to see who might have followed us out of town. I'll sleep a little during Delaware's watch if I'm lucky."

"Wake me at midnight, Bjorn," and with that Delaware, retrieved his bedroll from Cook's wagon, checked the ground for rocks, and lay down under the wagon with his back to the firelight.

Red greeted him when Bjorn came to him on his way out to patrol the outside area. He nuzzled the pocket where Bjorn usually kept some kind of a morsel for the animal, not easy do out on the trail like this. Taking his pointer finger, Bjorn reached for the horse's head and gently rubbed down from forehead to nose. A soft nickering came from the roan. Leaving Red, he headed for the outside perimeter of Stone's circled wagon train. "Larger groups must travel together," thought Bjorn, and then he saw two as he looked out. Other wagon trains had established their circles west up the river, closer to one of the forks. About one hundred feet of open area separated this train from the tree line behind them and the high grass where the trail led west toward the mountain range they'd have to cross. Another set of ruts closer to the tree line were signs that larger groups had stopped in this spot too. Up the river in open areas to the west like this one, Bjorn spotted three other groups, each an entity to themselves with fire pits forming the central part of their wheel.

Near the tree-lined edge, Bjorn noticed Stone questioning two of his wagon masters whose wagons were closest to the other caravan, apparently on their way to visit this group. Unsure of the outcome, Bjorn watched Stone firmly indicate to the two men that they needed to go back to their wagons. The men's voices grew louder as they argued. The river's rushing water muffled most sounds. Bjorn couldn't hear what was said but he saw the friction in the three bodies. Bjorn put his hand on his gun, ready to defend Stone if needed. Both men hesitated and, seeing him closing the space between with gun in hand, turned and headed back to the wagons they'd left unattended.

Night was filled with a variety of New World sounds, sounds not necessarily identifiable by Bjorn. The river amplified the woman's voice sweetly singing to a fiddle playing at one of the campsites along its banks. Bjorn walked closer and saw through an opening in their wagon fence a group gathered around the cooking fire no different than the one in Stone's camp. "Men must have been looking for entertainment. Can't blame them," thought Bjorn. "Probably looking for a wife too." Pausing in the shadows of the trees, Bjorn could see some dancing.

Others sat and listened, enjoying the last of the coffee provided.

Moving around the outside perimeter, Bjorn passed close to another wagon group. Here, a light hung inside one of the wagons, providing the shadow on the taut canvas of a mother trying to stifle the cry of an infant. Turning, Bjorn heard Red nicker and saw the roan was following him as best he could on the inside of the circle as he walked the outside. The horse's ears perked and so did Bjorn's attention when he saw the Red's reaction. All his mountain herding taught him animals were better to sense intrusion quicker than a human. Red's continued soft nickering brought a large, dappled grey horse out of the woods, one that Bjorn had seen earlier in the day tied to the back of one of the wagons. He was careful not to spook it as he worked his way towards the escapee, not wanting it to flee back into the wooded area behind. Close enough now to grab the trailing reins, Bjorn grasped them and headed back to camp with the horse in tow. Once inside the corral, Bjorn took a rope and tethered the horse near the cook's wagon. "Someone will find the wanderer in the morning," decided Bjorn. "No sense in waking everyone to see whose horse it is. Morning will do just fine."

Returning outside the circled boundary again in the area between wagon train and trees, Bjorn watched a woman move towards the wooded area, apparently wishing to take care of her necessaries. He decided to stay close, in view of the tree line but at a distance enough so that she could have her privacy. If she called for help for any reason, he would be close.

Time crawled as owls hooted, coyotes howled and horses neighed due to their restlessness from being penned in a strange area. The few pigs that were a part of the livestock snorted, all adding to the rest of the New World's strange sounds unfamiliar to him. Reaching the wooded area as he circled again and away from the river side, Bjorn heard a thrashing and used a sturdy, good sized tree for protection. He sighted his gun in the direction of the oncoming intruder and waited. Soon a small white head could be seen and Bjorn realized it was a lamb, seeking its mother. Looking at the moon's relationship to the horizon, Bjorn decided that his watch was over so he picked up the lamb, tucked it under his arm as he had done many times in the Nordic mountains, and headed back to the cook's wagon, wondering if its owner would be found or if it would be meat for tonight's stew.

"Short night for you too?" asked Bjorn of Cook, already busy preparing food for the new day.

"Need to get noon meal ready. No leftovers yet." He took one look at Bjorn with the lamb under his arm and reached for it, handed it to Delaware with the instructions, "Find the owner if you can or bring it back cleaned."

Reaching for the struggling, loudly complaining lamb, Delaware asked Bjorn, "Anything I should be aware of?"

"*Nei*, only the horse that I found wandering now tethered there in the center. Saw it yesterday tied to the back of one of the wagons but don't know whose. Not used to the night sounds here yet. Hope I didn't miss anything important."

"Stone?"

"Saw him once just as I was beginning to make rounds." Smiling he said, "He encouraged two of the men to go back to their wagons and not join the dancing at one of the other circles. Trains up and down the river, some larger, some smaller. All with a center campfire like ours, I think. Wake me if you need to."

Bjorn did as Delaware had done – grabbed his bed roll out of the cook's wagon and laid it down where Delaware's had been, now rolled and stashed behind Wind. He drank some coffee to satiate his thirst and washed his hands and face, using the pan and water jug at the back of the wagon along for that purpose. Exhausted from a long day and a longer evening on watch both filled with newness and uncertainty, Bjorn fell asleep as soon as he lay on his bedroll and didn't wake until he smelled the bacon and fried potatoes Cook was busy making for the morning meal.

"Eat quickly, Laddie. Need to get packed so we can be on the move. Think we want to make Haggerstown tonight," assumed Cook. "At least that's where we've stopped on the other trips out."

"Bacon and fried potatoes. What could be better over an open campfire? Hope we get lamb stew tonight," declared Bjorn feeling a little homesick. Finishing his breakfast, he took his tin plate to the back of the cook's wagon and saw the pile of dirty dishes piled on the bench. He washed his cup and plate, then continued washing the pots and pans stacked at the side on the bench.

"Help's appreciated," noted Cook as he added one more to the dwindling stack. "Fresh meat's always welcome but takes time away from packing to leave. Stone's fair, like we said, but gets really grumbly if Delaware and I don't make a good example for the others, so we need to pack fast and be ready for the trail."

"Haven't been told to do otherwise, so I'll stay here and help you." An appreciative look came from Cook as he hurried back to the front of the wagon to stow more of his supplies.

Packing meant finishing the washing of pots and pans, placing them in the barrel, anchoring the cover so it wouldn't come free, loading the water barrels in case water was not available at the next top, filling the tinder box, and finding enough dried wood to make a decent cooking fire. As Cook was finishing the stowing, Bjorn harnessed Cook's draft horse to the rung, saddled Red and rode off to find either Stone or Delaware and get more instructions for his duties. Both were talking to Hiram whose wagon was almost empty since most of his provisions were lost in the river crossing fiasco of yesterday.

"We should make Haggerstown tonight. You can resupply there," came from Stone with a firmness in his voice.

"Not sure I have the cash to do so. Lost so much," mumbled Hiram, head hanging down.

"You've a strong back. Stay there. Work a while and get what you need. Catch on with another train when you're ready. There's always one going west. You learned a hard lesson." With that Stone turned, motioned for Hiram to get in line, and ordered Delaware to continue to watch the train move out.

Stone signaled to the lead cart to head down the path and indicated to Bjorn to "ride the rear." Wheels squeaked and dust clouds formed, but the smoothness in which the mass of wagons, animals, and people on foot wended their way down the well-worn trail ahead surprised Bjorn who'd expected to be delayed by someone dallying.

Chapter 12

"Ready to meet the Yaocomico?" probed Delaware.

"Yaocomico? Who're they?" questioned Bjorn. The two rode quite a ways ahead of the train, scouting the trail for difficult crossings and other dangers.

"Peaceful group of natives. Scare the living devil out of new arrivals."

"Why's that? Come raiding?"

"It's the tattoos. Bodies are painted different colors. Tattoos and manmade beads decorate their bodies."

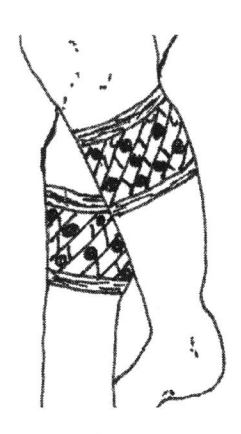

"Why are we meeting them?" Once again he wondered what he had gotten himself in to deciding to follow his dream.

"Need to barter with them for their corn, beans and squash – see if they've any cured venison or jerky."

"Must be a friendly group," was Bjorn's comment.

"*Ja,*" offered Delaware with a smile. "Don't be surprised if you hear rattles, drums or flutes coming from the woods. The handmade instruments are part of their celebrating."

Looking to his left and the open flatland that began to rise off the trail, he said, "Looks like we're headed into the mountains."

"We follow the Potomac or one of its feeders, Hamilton Run or Antietam Creek, not quite sure which way Stone has chosen."

"More fording?" asked Bjorn, wanting to be ready for the next crossing.

"Not sure. Depends on the way Stone wants to go this time."

"Haggerstown? A big town?"

"Not too big. Town has stone ridges made of limestone running through it. It's why Stone told Hiram he could stay and find work. Chunks of limestone are hauled by cart or wagon back east to build stone buildings."

"You speak the Yaocomico language, Delaware?"

"Enough so I can trade. Might have to build a travois to bring the supplies back to the cook's wagon."

"Travois? Some kind of a cart?"

"Forget you're not native, Bjorn. You seem so at ease out here. We'll make two by taking long trailing poles or poles that have brush or ropes connecting them if we can't find sturdy ones. Have to anchor them with rope and lash them securely to our horse trappings. We'll spread the poles wider at the base so that items can be hauled that way. We'll wrap what we barter in cured skins like this one tied behind here," and he pointed to the pack behind his saddle. "The make-shift cart is dragged behind."

He finished his explanation just as a Yaocomico brave stepped out of the forest area along the trail. Raising his right hand up in greeting, Delaware said, "Rook, glad to see you."

"Too," came from Rook as he shifted his gaze to Bjorn and his head of curly blond hair.

"Bjorn, new scout. Going to the Territories."

Bjorn moved Red slowly forward and extended his arm bent at the elbow with the hand up to the brave, aware now of the tattoos on arms and legs. Making eye contact, both touched palms. Accepting the presence of the intruder, Rook turned and led the two on horse to his village.

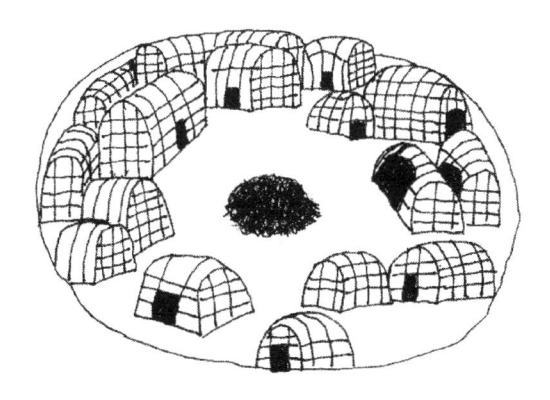

The village was bigger than Bjorn expected, though as he thought about it, he had no idea what to expect here in the New World. These natives lived in small oval houses with roofs and walls made of woven reeds. The structures were arranged in a circle with a fire pit in its center, very similar to the circled wagons.

Young braves stood at the entrance of the village, ready to care for their horses. Delaware dismounted and so did Bjorn, each handing the reins of their mounts into the hands of the eager boys who began to curry and care for the three horses.

Bjorn's eyes widened when Rook led the two of them into the largest of the buildings. Tables arranged in long rows were laden with three varieties of squash. Beans that were still in their husks or shelled lay on another. One table held corn, dried on the cob. A smaller table to its left had leather bags of ground corn meal, one of the requests from some of the wagon master's wives when they heard Delaware was going for supplies.

Bjorn turned back towards the opening they'd entered, aware of giggles coming from the doorway. The gesturing and pointing to his hair and skin made him uncomfortable until he realized that these young girls had probably not seen many people with blonde curly hair like his. Nor had they seen as white a skin as his, still not tanned from the sun.

Delaware moved toward him, grinned and said, "Check the skins. Need five or so. Want to make *parfleches*." All he got from Bjorn was a dumb stare. "Forgot. A *parfleche* is a rawhide bag. It can be any size – a full animal skin used to wrap bed rolls or anything else that needs to be kept dry. I need five to make smaller ones to hold dried meat and *pemmican*. You need your own bed roll bag. Yours belongs to Stone."

Knowing the size of Delaware's medicine and jerky bags, Bjorn went to the table and examined the cured skins. The quality of the workmanship and the quantity of the skins piled high amazed him. Choosing six, one for himself, he took his choices back to where Delaware had the items he hoped to purchase.

Delaware was now on the other side of the long house, looking at the stripped poles leaning against the reed wall. Choosing four, he came back to the stacked table, leaned the sturdy poles along its side and continued over to the larger cured skins. "Must be looking for wraps for all we have bought so we can secure the supplies to the poles," floated through Bjorn's mind as he watched the inspection. Choices made, Delaware then moved to a smaller table where leather ties of all lengths lay. Checking for weak spots and consistency of the leather's width, he chose wisely and added to the stash. Last, he moved to the leather leggings and shirts, hung on the walls by wooden dowels and motioned to Bjorn to come closer. "Find a size that fits you. They will stretch a little when you wear them."

"How much?" came from Bjorn.

"Part of Stone's salary. He was quite impressed that you helped Cook pack, 'specially with the dishes."

"You choose for me. I'm your size. You know what's best."

Delaware chose a frontier style simply made legging and shirt, one that would be acceptable back at the wagon train and serviceable along the trail.

Moving back to the stacked table of supplies, Delaware in the halting, guttural native tongue of the Yaocomico asked that his roll behind his saddle be brought. When one of the young braves brought it to him, Delaware opened it, revealing sharpened hatchets, hammers, bottles of peppermint syrup, and tobacco. Eyes gleamed as various braves handled the hatchets and hammers. Tobacco found its way to the medicine man who quieted the braves by giving each one of the smaller linen parcels. Two were given to an elderly, aged grandmother whose toothless smile Bjorn was sure he'd never forget. What little remained was taken to the hut that must have been the shaman's.

With the trade completed, Delaware lost little time in rigging the two travois, anxious to return to the train already on the trail. Escorted out by Rook, the three parted friends and continued on their separate ways.

"Does all trading go that simply?" asked Bjorn, impressed by the ease Delaware had bartering.

"Been trading with them for four years or so. First trades were difficult. No trust. Once the Yaocomico know you won't steal or cheat them, they trade very fairly. Helps that I can fumble with their tongue."

With the travois behind, the time on the trail took much longer than their coming to the village. The two stopped frequently to be sure that the leather ropes were still tight and the load was secure.

"Lucky you're still with," came from Delaware.

"How so?"

"When I asked you to check the skins, I wasn't sure you even knew what a good skin should look like but I knew I needed to keep you away from those giggles. Any one of them would have been glad to take you back to their hut."

"We cure skins too, probably not the same way you do. I just wasn't sure how big or what animal skin I was looking at. Green, again!" replied Bjorn, realizing that he would be green for a long time, always learning, in this New World.

Chapter 13

Each day blended into the next as the train made its way along the trail under Stone's guidance. Respect for him grew as small squabbles were settled fairly and with little discipline enforced. Hiram chose to stay in Haggerstown and work, but his bullheadedness and disobeying orders were memories each wagon master had and did not want to duplicate. The cargo of each wagon was precious to its owner and in some cases not replaceable out here in the wild wilderness. Sacks or barrels of potatoes, beans, beets, onions and turnips were staples in most wagons. Keeping flour and rice dry caused the most problems. Rain could do just as much damage as fording a river.

Oxen and their carts crossed the smaller tributaries easily. If a driver sensed that his load was too heavy, those behind helped him unload so that the oxen could easily walk across the rocky riverbeds. Unloaded items were then carried by hand to the other side rather than returning the wagon and reloading. Time was saved this way. Children and sometimes the women folk were carried across too. When the water was swifter, a neighbor would double-up his team of oxen with another to help speed the process of getting everyone's wagon across.

Once across and closer to the community settlement in front of them, the lush, level land of the Medina farming country intrigued two of the wagon masters whose wives were tired of the constant pack and unpack each evening. Small acreage was available so both families asked for permission to leave the train. The two families were bee keepers in the Old Country, coming from Gottenburg, Sweden, and were hoping to continue keeping bees here in the New World.

Stone returned part of their payment he'd received for the complete guidance to Carter's Cove and wished them well. Both parties moved off the trail to a secluded spot protected on one side by a small grove of trees but faced open land in full floral bloom. They each had a small hive with them, cared for them daily. One of the wives spotted toad trillium in the woods with its deep maroon flowers that smelled like raw beef. The bright yellow flowers just beginning to bloom in the prairie grass the other wife recognized as black-eyed susans, just like those she remembered from the pastures back home.

The wagon masters knew if their wives were happy, the prospect of claiming land would be easier for all. "Stone's having the train camp here a night or two," one of the men offered to the other. "Gives us a chance to look around."

"Need to see if the community will let us mix our dark bees with their different strain," the other cautioned. "Keep the lids on the boxes until we know."

Once they'd settled for the night, the two went to the merchant's store and sought information about available land and permission to join the bee keeping community. The rest of the caravan spent time with Stone's permission replacing supplies, so needed by many. Some had not anticipated well what would be needed and their original stash was exhausted. When Delaware met with Rook and the Yaocomico, others weren't interested in trading with the Indians so their supplies were drained. Taking a break in the relentless daily moving, the families met at campfires and talked, beneficial when one person needed help from another.

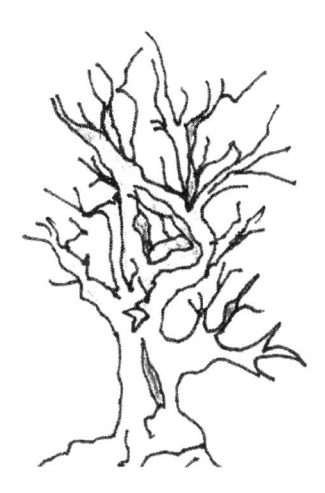

"Mama!" screamed a small child holding her hand over her eye, coming back from the wooded perimeter and taking care of her necessaries. "Mama!" she yelled with pain in her voice.

"You've been stung by a bee. Did you throw something at their hive in the tree?" Hives hung in the trees along the edge of the open grassland filled with a rainbow of flowers.

"No, I was careful, just like you said. I think it was in the grass beside the trench. Take the pain away, please mama," wailed the young girl.

Taking a rag from her stash and wetting it with water from her barrel, mom handed it to the girl. "Hold this cool cloth over you eye. I need to get my ointment" and began to frantically search in her wood box that had the *cures* in it.

"What happened?" asked Delaware, riding up to see what had upset the child.

"Stung by a bee. Can't find the ointment," came from the flustered mother of the weeping child.

Reaching into his side pack, Delaware extracted a small sac that had comfrey leaves in it. "Make a poultice of meal and water. Mix the leaves in. Should draw the bee poison out and make the swelling go down. Take some of the pain away too."

Forgetting to say thanks – so concerned for her daughter, the woman took the sac and quickly mixed the concoction. She placed a bit on the swollen area, and gave the girl a precious sugar lump to suck on, hoping to distract her as well as ease the pain.

Next morning, the train moved out, headed for a peninsula located along Lake Erie called Cedar Point.

"Find Oar," order Stone. Delaware knew what that meant.

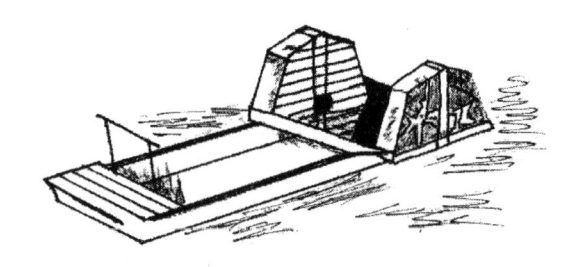

"Why do we need to find an oar? We don't have a boat with us, do we?" was Bjorn's query when the two were on the trail headed west.

"Oar has two good sized rafts that are powered by wheels on a rope and pulley system. Stone has an arrangement with him to transport his train from Sandusky to Port Clinton. Oar needs to know we're coming so that he hasn't made other agreements with other wagon masters."

"Are we close to Port Clinton?" asked Bjorn, curious to know where they were headed. "A day's ride for the train, less by horseback if we high tail it. Don't need to do that. Cedar is a wonderful fishing port. Those who want to fish can do so later tonight for a change in diet. Those who can afford it, can buy fresh and smoked fish from the locals."

"Wouldn't mind a good fish stew," came from Bjorn, remembering time past in the Nordic mountains that had the stream at their base. Fishing was always good.

"You'll get your wish. Cook stocks up on smoked fish. Less bulk to carry than other meat. Makes a good stew too," revealed Delaware.

Bjorn thought the trail was long and endless today. His mouth already watered with the thought of fish stew. Rounding the bend laden with overhanging trees, the two riders came to the banks of the river. Looking out, they saw the barge-like float being pulled to the other side, heaped with lumber. "Think we have a wait, right?

"You're right. Just missed Oar. I'll see if I can't get his attention so he knows we're here. Might hurry him up a little to get back. Might not. He's a mind of his own, much like Hiram," came from Delaware as he handed his horse's reins to Bjorn. "Water them and tether them. Grass is lush along the bank. A nice treat for them."

Dismounting and taking the reins of the two horses, Bjorn led them to the river's edge, allowed them to drink and then tethered them to a good sized young tree and the available fresh grass below it. Horses attended, Bjorn went to the river bank and stripped. First he washed his clothes and laid them on the rocks to dry. Then he swam to wash his body. Both dried quickly by the sun's heat on the rock overlooking the river, affected by the noon day sun. Redressing later, Bjorn stretched out as best he could on the rock shelf and waited for Delaware to either join him or give him more instructions.

Bees buzzing lulled Bjorn to sleep. Next thing he knew, he woke to the smell of meat sizzling over an open fire. Embarrassed that he had been so lax, he walked over to where Oar and Delaware were seated. Introductions made, Bjorn softly spoke. "Green again. I'll try harder next time to be more attentive. Should I be doing something?"

"*Nei*," offered Delaware. "Train will soon be here. Hear the squeaking? Think we need to go frog hunting." Without pausing, he continued, "Took Oar longer than usual to unload the wood and reload the furniture destined for the bigger community west of here just starting to build wood structures."

"Didn't make another trip. I'll haul the rest of that stack you see piled over tomorrow. Decided to wait until the caravan got here. Save my back for the trips hauling across the river," said Oar, flexing his arms to relieve tension.

"Frog hunting? Are we going fishing?" questioned Bjorn.

"No. Need grease for those squeaky oxcart wheels. Don't suppose they have too much of that left. Most of it was used to come over the higher mountain-like passes. Frogs will do in a pinch."

"Learn something every day," thought Bjorn as he took the wooden pail offered and headed for the swamp-like bank farther down. Catching frogs was easy. Keeping them in the bucket proved more of a challenge. Oar laughed as the two struggled, and then he handed both a flat, dented tin plate that had seen much use. Each plate fit just inside the bucket and worked as a lid for the pail.

With their buckets full and sitting on the ground waiting, both watched as the wagons circled without being told, smaller ahead of the larger, heavier ones. "Take the buckets to the last in line. Have them start greasing their axels. Cook's got two more pails in his wagon. Take them and fill them too. See that each wagon greases up. The next stop is Mount Baldy." Leaving Bjorn, Delaware went off to find Stone to get his instructions for the crossing which would begin once all wheels were greased.

"Frogs! Why're you giving me a bucket of frogs?" came from the man whose wagon was last in line. "Am I to go fishing?"

"*Nei*, need to grease your wheels. Have any grease in your wagon?" responded Bjorn.

"No. Used the last on that steep descent two days ago."

"Our next stop is Mount Baldy. Wheels need to be ready for it," stated Bjorn like he knew what crossing Mount Baldy was all about.

He continued to hand buckets to the wagon masters who had not made the effort to get grease out and use it to grease the wagon wheels. One or two had enough sense to go to the same marshy place Bjorn was using to get their own frogs to use. When he'd completed his task of delivering frogs to those in need, he went back to one of the wagons where a woman was struggling, trying to get a wheel off her small ox cart.

"Ma'am, need some help?" asked Bjorn.

Tears flowed as the fortyish woman looked gratefully at Bjorn. "Thought I could do this. Used to hard work. Wheel seems to have a mind of its own. Didn't know I needed grease. And the frogs . . . don't think I can kill them." She buried her tear-stained face in her hands, her elbows resting on her knees as she sat back on her haunches.

Bjorn gently touched her shoulder, helped her up and out of the way and continued the task of removing the wheel from the axel, took his knife and punctured each frog at the base of its throat as he placed one after the other around the hub casing in the same way he would have if what he was using were grease. He completed the task just in time for her wagon's turn to be loaded on the barge. The ox stood patiently, waiting to be led across.

"How can I pay you? I have very little. If you need clothes washed or mended, I'd be happy to do that. That was my job before I left home," spoke the woman with gratefulness in her voice.

"No pay necessary. We all need help now and again." Bjorn helped her get her cart on the barge. "You ride over too. I'll lead your ox over for you." Returning from seeing the woman's cart off the scow, he went down the line to see if others needed help.

Last in line was a four-wheeled wagon, laden with heavy furniture and who knew what else. Sitting on the bench up front was a gentleman who wore a black suit – at least it used to be until all the trail dust gave it a dark red color. Bjorn quickly recognized him as the one always complaining about his position in the line. This crossing was no different for him. "Bjorn, Why'm I always last? I've told Stone I'd pay extra to be farther up in the line. Hate all this dust."

"Price you pay for having the heaviest load and largest rig." Pausing a moment as he looked at the overloaded four-wheeled wagon pulled by two larger than usual draft horses, Bjorn continued to comment, "Think you'll have to make two trips. Might as well start unloading so that only the wagon makes the first trip. Then you need to lead the team over. Oar will divide the load and bring it over in two trips. That way you can reload easier as you take your belongings off the raft."

"Won't do that. Going to take the loaded wagon over just as it is. Isn't that heavy," declared the determined fellow.

"Do as Bjorn said, Jenson," was heard from Stone who come up behind Bjorn and was listening to the instructions. "Do as he said or stay on this side and find a place to live here. Oar doesn't need his raft sunk by the likes of you."

Both Bjorn and Stone left the man and rode to the edge of the riverbank. "Take this last crossing, Bjorn. There's room for Red and you." Bjorn looked back at the fellow they'd left. "He'll come. Nothing here for him. Needs to be somewhere like Chicago or Carter's Cove where he'll be able to push his weight around. He's got a lot of weight to push, that one."

Chapter 14

Morning found Bjorn up early, using a slice of fresh bread to lap up the last of the fish stew leftovers Cook offered him from last night's meal. Knowing how much Bjorn loved fish, especially fish stew, Cook saved the dregs from the cooking pot. "Appreciate this."

"Least I can do," said Cook. "Help me when it isn't even your duty. See a pile of dishes and you tackle them before you ride out to see what Stone or Delaware has for you to do. Wish I could meet your Ma. Must be a fine lady to train you like she has."

"Mor and Far taught Erik and me work was work. Wasn't his work or her work but work. I imagine Anna is learning that now too." Finishing his breakfast, Bjorn took his plate, scraped the fish bones into a garbage bucket, already heaping and ready to be dumped and buried. Rolling up his shirt sleeves, he began the task of washing the stack of pots, pans, and tinware that Stone, Delaware, Cook and he had dirtied. As fast as he could wash, Cook used a ragged shirt that had more holes than material to wipe and store each item for the trip to Mount Baldy and beyond.

Finished and still curious about this Mount Baldy, Bjorn saddled Red and rode to where Delaware was helping tie down a pump organ in a smaller ox cart. "Make sure the box is in the center of the cart," instructed Delaware. "Might make the load more stable and less likely to tumble out when we go over the dunes."

"Morning," came from Bjorn as he rode up to the small cart and oxen.

"Just coming to look for you. Need to ride and check how the dunes have shifted since last time we were here," voiced Delaware.

The two began their usual morning duty of checking the trail ahead, sometimes reporting back to Stone if a trail change was necessary because a certain portion of it had deep ruts or pot holes that needed to be avoided. At other times, the two were free to fish or hunt for game to replenish Cook's supply. When the catch was plentiful, Bjorn and Delaware passed out fresh fillets to wagon families that found themselves lacking meat for the evening meal. Ambling down the trail riding through lush grass that reached the haunches of the horses, Bjorn asked, "Dunes. What are these dunes?"

"Mount Baldy rises from the lake shore and eventually to Shikaakwa, the Chicago River portage that connects to Mud Lake. We'll follow it until we get to the part of Stinky Onion where some of my relatives, the Algonquin, live. The trail follows rivers that will take us to Carter's Cove."

Scratching his head in confusion, Bjorn mouthed, "Baldy? Stinky Onion? And you think the names we have back in the Old Country are strange!"

"Baldy is not the same kind of mountain where you herded sheep. Baldy is a sand dune about 125 feet tall that moves."

"Moves? A mountain moves?" came from Bjorn with uncertainty in his voice.

"*Ja.*" Delaware smiled. "Winds blowing off the lake cause the sand to drift, sometimes so much that it buries trees and whatever else is in its path. That's why we need to check the trail."

"Will we have to do any clearing?"

"Don't think so. When the sand moves, it leaves a solid base until that base begins to rise up the mountain. If we have trouble, it will be from those who do not stay on the trail and get in the softer sand. Michiana can be both kind and evil that way."

"Michiana?"

"Sorry," Delaware uttered. "Michiana is the Miami or Illinois name for the mountain, used by the older people in the tribe who think the mountain speaks too."

"Stinky Onion. Is that a real onion or another name for something?" continued Bjorn as the two rode leisurely along on a part of the trail that moved through low lying brush laden with early spring berries

"Shikaakawa. Miami word for the Chicago River that we'll follow until it meets the Mississippi. Plants along the river look somewhat like onions and smell like them so the tribe calls the river Stinky Onion."

"So when I smell onion, I'll know I'm there."

"My people live on both sides of the Mississippi up ahead. Need to visit them when we get there. Need to see my *okomisan*. Grandmother raised me when my mother died from small pox and my father was killed in a battle."

"His people must be the Algonquian," decided Bjorn, who had read as much as he could find about the New World Indian people. Would one of Delaware's relatives help him get to Old Crossing? What a boon that would be to have someone who knew the territory lead him.

Baldy loomed ahead now. "I'll have to see if Leif and Helmer need help. They won't know much about crossing shifting sand," decided Bjorn. It was the least he could do for them. Had he not seen them when he came off the schooner and been guided to this wagon train, would he have been so lucky? First to have Stone allow him free passage with the train for his scouting. Second to have made such a good friend as Delaware who he would trust with his life. Third to find out that Delaware's people lived along the Mississippi, the river that ran north to where he needed to go.

Reaching the base of the dune that ran next to the lakeshore, Delaware pointed left and sent Bjorn to ride the trail, looking for soft spots. "Ride about an hour and check the trail. It is not the usual one we use. It's longer and winds through more of the city. Rather not take the train that way but need to have an alternative if Mud Lake is mud." The lake could be wet, dry or marshy depending upon how much snow melt and rain the area had received.

Delaware rode to the right, checking the trail to see if it would be smarter to go his way. He hadn't ridden far when a palomino came racing towards him, rider leaning over the animal's mane and using it as a bridle. Joy filled his heart. And then fear. Why was River here? Was grandmother ill?

Slowing when reaching Delaware, both dismounted and embraced. "Trouble?" came in a whisper from Delaware.

"No, Wise Woman sent me. Knew you were near. Wanted me to protect you from the spirits of the mountain" and he handed Delaware a beaded pouch, one Delaware recognized as one of his grandmother's medicine bags.

"The trail?" asked Delaware, knowing River had just traversed the route.

"One mud spot. Only the heaviest of wagons will find difficulty. Rest won't need to unload.

"Glad we left Jenson behind. Don't need his kind of trouble."

"Jenson? Trouble?"

"Big four-wheeled wagon, heavily loaded, driven by four large draft horses. Independent sort too. Didn't like riding last in line. Did not like to take orders."

"Don't need those kind out here in the wilderness" was River's decision from the little he knew about the fellow and his family.

As the two rode side by side back to where the trail met the base of the mountain, River wanted to know, "Leave others behind?"

"One fellow couldn't wait for his turn, headed for the river bank. Horses and wagon got caught in an eddy and sinkhole. Wagon contents floated down the river. Had little left and less means to buy replacements. Decided to work for a while and catch another train going west."

"One? That all? Must be a good group."

"Two other families. Bee keepers. Women were not prepared for the hard trail. Both stopped at Medina where there are other families who raise bees."

"Cook and Stone?"

"Cook has been much better on this trip. Bjorn signed on just off the ship from the Old Country. Sheep herder. Knows horses too. Isn't afraid of work. Isn't particular what kind of work. Has washed a lot of pots and pans," offered Delaware, aware that men doing women's work was not highly thought of by the native tribe. "Very accurate with a sling shot. Has brought many a small squirrel and fox back to Cook."

"Stone?"

"Same. Hardnosed but fair."

Reaching the lakeshore, Delaware untied one of his smaller saddle bags and let his horse roam freely knowing one whistle would bring Wind back instantly. "Help me catch a fish or two. Got line? Bjorn won't be back for a while. Told him to ride out and check the other trail. Didn't know how much mud we faced."

Chapter 15

Bjorn returned from his trail inspection and found Delaware and another person, relatively the same age and wearing the same beaded markings on his leather leggings and shirt, busy fishing the shallows of the lake where water swirled. Behind them on the shore far enough so the flopping fish could not find their way back to the water lay twenty large pink salmon, as big a fish as any Bjorn had seen caught in the river at home.

"Want to fish or clean?" came from Delaware as Bjorn dismounted. "We've had fun. Salmon are running. River and I haven't had so much luck fishing since we were young braves."

"Fish, I think. I've probably skinned and cleaned more lambs and you more fish," offered Bjorn. "I'd waste a lot of the fish. Not sure where the bones are."

"Need to dry a few too. *Okomisan* will be unhappy if we don't bring her one or two," said River.

Calling a halt to the fishing, Delaware asked, "Bjorn, see if you can find some dry firewood so we can smoke these." Bjorn put his fishing line away and wandered down the shore to a deadfall that was partly submerged. When he took them back the wet, board-like pieces of driftwood became planking so that fish fillets could lay beside the fire and cure.

On his way back to the fallen tree, he picked scattered fragments of the tree until his hands were filled. Returning with the first load of smaller sticks and leaves, he took his flint and lit the tinder he'd placed in the center under the few larger pieces that he'd arranged in a teepee fashion. The other two continued to clean fish.

The smoldering tinder greeted him when Bjorn came with his second load. Adding this load to the fire, he went searching again for larger pieces, knowing that more wood would be needed to cook the fish. Much more aware of sounds in this New World now, Bjorn ears perked when he picked the last piece of driftwood for this pile in his arms. All too familiar sounds of the wheels squeaking rumbled in the wind, signaling that the wagon train was about an hour away. Cook would be pleased to find fresh fish cleaned and ready for tonight's meal.

"Bjorn, need you," came from Stone as the train rode into the secluded area along the lake. Baldy loomed in front of them, winds moving the sand. Those closer to the perimeter and walking barefoot as many did to save their shoes for a more needed time felt a gentle pelting at the ankles.

Quickly saddling Red, Bjorn loped to where Stone watched the wagon train circle in their now very familiar pattern. "What can I do for you?"

"Simple. Be my eyes and ears. Need to know if anyone's wheels are giving them trouble from all this sand. Also need to know if anyone's sick. Check on that lady with the small cart and see how she is doing, the one you helped a while back. Helmer's son, Rolf, sprained an ankle I think or broke it. Tripped over a vine just now hidden in the shifting sand. See how he's doing. Find me later tonight. I need to talk to River and Delaware. Need to decide the best route to get around or across the Chicago. Not enough experienced wagon masters in this group so need to be careful which way we go. Oh, and send one per family to get fish for supper if you caught enough. Nice surprise." Satisfied that he'd covered most of what needed to be taken care of, Stone turned and headed for the two braves tending the fish and fire at the edge of Cook's wagon.

As he circled the train, Bjorn stopped at each wagon. While he spoke to the wagon master of each cart or wagon, he also looked as best he could to see how the family unit was faring. Some he spent more time with than others. Some were more willing to talk. Most were grateful someone cared enough to check on them. The women particularly smiled when they heard his parting words, "Send someone to the Cook's wagon for salmon."

Helmer found him before Bjorn got to his wagon. "Know anything about setting bones, Bjorn?"

"*Nei*," don't. How bad is it?"

"One is almost ready to break skin. Been asking. Don't have a doctor."

"Go ask Delaware. Never know. Might be able to help."

"*Nei*. Could you? I get nervous when I speak English."

Or was he hesitant to speak to him because Delaware was an Indian? Bjorn didn't know but turned Red back towards the Cook's wagon to where River and Delaware were handing out parcels of salmon to each who came for their share. Looking up, Delaware mouthed so that those close could not hear, "Trouble?"

"*Nei*. Need someone to set Rolf's bone in the leg. Helmer's wondering if either of you know anything about that."

"River does. He's watched *Okomisan* more than me," and he turned, traded places with River and spoke to him in their native language so that the rest of the train would not worry. Least that's what the two thought. Eyes turned to both the braves when those around heard the strange language, wondering what was being planned and unsure if there was danger they should be aware of in the area.

"Don't worry, people. I've asked River to see to Rolf's ankle. He's been around his grandmother when she's had some experience in doing this." A sigh of relief came from those closest as they continued to collect their salmon and head back to their wagon.

"Where'm I going?" River wanted to know, now on foot, walking alongside Red.

"Hiram and Leif are people from my country. Families are going where I hope to go, I think. Rolf, Hiram's son, tripped on a vine and broke a bone in his ankle. About to cut through the skin. Hope you can help."

"See what I can do. Need my medicine bag on the left side near my pommel. Will need some water and a little of Cook's dry oatmeal, about a small handful. Need a small bowl too."

Reaching Helmer's wagon, the two found Rolf, lying in the back with his britches pushed above the knee and his sock off exposing the leg. Some of their belongings were strewn on the ground so he could comfortably lay in the wagon bed. Pain radiated from his face as he strained not to shed unmanly tears. River looked at the area that was already swelling and discoloring. "Will need you and his father once you go get my bag and the rest." Glad that he had listened to his grandmother and learned to speak the English, he began the process of making the young lad feel as much at ease as he could, knowing he'd probably never had an Indian this close nor had one touch him. Running his hand on the opposite side of the protruding bump, River questioned, "Hurt on this side?"

"*Nei.*"

Moving his hand around to the back side of the ankle area he asked, "Here?"

"*Ja*. Liten."

Moving to the side where the bone looked to be most separated, River pointed instead of touching. "Here?"

"*Ja*. Liten," came from Rolf as Bjorn returned with River's medicine bag, the oatmeal, a tin cup and some warm water.

Opening his bag, River removed a small packet of crumbled birch bark and placed it in the warm water to soften. When the crumbles softened, he added a little oatmeal and stirred the two items into a paste. Looking at the mother who was standing at the side of the wagon, ringing her hands, River said, "Need a clean rag to wrap."

Reaching for a close, smaller barrel, she opened it and removed a white bandage she's prepared much earlier before they'd left the Old Country. "She prepared just for such an emergency," Bjorn thought.

"Here," came from her in a whisper.

"Bjorn, hop in wagon. Lean over Rolf at his shoulders. Helmer, hold other leg down." Both men took their positions. Looking at Bjorn, River queried, "Know what to do?"

"*Ja*. Done this before," came from the steady voice of Bjorn.

"Ready?" One jerk was all it took and the bone was back in place as screams of pain came from Rolf held down by both men. Once Rolf's agony subsided some, both men released their holds on him. River took the poultice he had made, covered the bruising area and wrapped the ankle with the bandage. "Can't walk on this foot. Needs to heal. First moon you ride back here. Then use a crutch for six moons. Should heal by then."

"*Tukk*," came from the sweat covered face of the lad.

Handing the mother what he had left of the ground birch bark in the small pouch and the rest of the oatmeal that hadn't been used, he said, "Shouldn't need this after the next two nights. If it swells, find me," and he walked back to the cook's wagon where Delaware sat by the fire eating his salmon meal.

Bjorn continued his inspection as instructed. Only other person that was struggling as he moved from wagon to wagon was the same woman whose cart wheels he'd greased with the frogs. With her backside to the ox, she tried to lift the right front hoof of the animal. It wasn't cooperating at all. "Sore foot?"

"Suspect she's a stone caught. Won't let me look."

Dismounting, Bjorn took the place of the woman, lifted the hoof up so he could examine it and saw she was right. A stone had lodged. Taking his knife he always carried on his belt, he carefully removed the stone, released the hoof, and rubbed the oxen's nose. It snorted a little and then brayed loudly as though it was thanking Bjorn. "That should do it."

"Again I owe you. You've yet to collect from the first time you helped me with the wheels."

"You'll get your chance to help someone along the way. That will be payment for me."

She extended her hand. "I'll remember that and make sure I do. What is this Mud Lake that we have in front of us?"

"Don't know. Never been there either. Need to trust Stone. This is where Delaware and River are from. Their people, their families live not far from here. They'll help us get through. It's dry. Haven't had much rain here lately to make it muddy. We're lucky, I think. Need to check the rest of the train and get a piece of the salmon before it's all gone. Haven't had any since I left the Old Country."

Morning came early and each of the wagon masters was busy tying down the reloaded possessions, filling water casks, and harnessing the horses or oxen for the trek through Mud Lake.

Fear hung around all of them. Mud lake. No one wanted to get mired down, one of the most difficult situations for a wagon, ox cart or, for that matter, an animal. If a wheel buried itself to the hub, they'd have to detach the horse or oxen from the wagon and men lifted and pulled the rope attached around the axel until the wagon came free. When pulling didn't free the wagon, scythes came out from their storage places. The long grasses along the banks were cut and braided or twisted into knots. Lifting each wheel, one at a time, the wads of grass were placed under and the men pulled again. The pattern repeated itself until the wagon was free. No one wanted to be mired in the muck so all heeded Stone's instructions.

"Bjorn, take the day and go with Delaware and River. Need to see this land you're so anxious to settle on. Need to see how they live," he said, pointing to the two braves. "Lake is dry so we shouldn't have trouble. See you tonight," and he turned and rode to the head of the train.

Chapter 16

Each horse appeared to know the other's whereabouts as the three loped along the trail ahead of the train. The salmon wrapped in a *parfleche* was tied just behind their saddles. Little was said. Little needed to be. The beauty of the landscape entranced Bjorn. Grass grew greener and taller than he'd ever seen it. Flowers bloomed, bees and birds sang, and small animals scurried to the edges of the trail as the horses approached.

Arrow and Pierce, two young braves who were sentinels for River's village, came loping towards them. "Okomisan's worried. Thought something happened to you," said Arrow to them as he eyed Bjorn riding last in line. Setting the horses to jogging, the five were greeted and guided into the center by most of those who were not out gathering food to replace the winter's use.

This village had the same small oval houses with walls made of woven reeds similar to the other village Bjorn had visited with Delaware. "Wonder when I'll see homes made from animal skins like all the pictures in the books that I was able to read?" he thought.

In the center of the oval of houses a group of men worked around a stack of birch trees, logged from the woods that boarded the trail in to the homes. Their attention focused on building a canoe. Bjorn watched as the men, using a wooden wedge, pried off ten to twelve foot nine inch or so wide sections of the bark. The peeled-off sections were stuck together with a resin from balsam fir trees he was told later. The same resin was spread over the outside of the bark, giving it a water proof effect. A finished canoe rested on its side not far from the one being built and Bjorn went to inspect it.

"Lift it," suggested River.

Bjorn did. "I'm surprised how light it is." Now he understood how portaging rivers looked so easy. There was so little weight to the canoe that one person could carry it if it were empty. He estimated it weighted no more than his little sister, about 40 or 50 pounds. The most amazing part was that there was room for four people, two sitting side by side on each of the two bench seats inside the canoe. "I'll have to remember to tell the folks back in the Old Country about these canoes when I next write to them," declared Bjorn. "They'll be amazed at how light weight they are." Walking over to another boat a distance from where the team of men were working, he saw a different style boat, made in a different way. A log that had been hollowed out, leaving a seat in front and back. "This

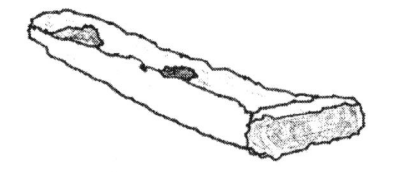

must be a trapper's boat or maybe a boat used for ricing," surmised Bjorn. It was much sturdier looking but also looked much heavier. Two poles and two long-handled paddles lay in the hollowed out portion of the boat. Standing, looking and marveling at the talents of the tribe who lacked many of the conventional tools Bjorn was used to, he was thankful for growing up where he had. He may not have the tools here in the New World but he'd had the experience of using them. Knowledge never hurt. Rattled from his dreaming, Bjorn reacted to the summons.

"Bjorn, come," motioned River as he stood outside what Bjorn presumed to be grandmother's reed-built house. "Come meet Wise Woman, *Okomisan,* my grandmother."

Stepping inside the house, Bjorn had little time to observe his surroundings. Grandmother motioned him to come and sit by her on a pile of skins next to a small fire pit where a pot simmered, hanging over low smoldering embers. Her face shone with pride when she pointed to Delaware and River. "Good sons."

"Good friends," offered Bjorn.

Lifting her hand to Bjorn's head, she stroked the unruly curls, now long and hanging near his shoulders. "Corn."

"She doesn't know the English word for yellow," chuckled Delaware. More words came from her, spoken to the two who sat on the other side of her. "She wants to know how you curl it. Wants to curl her hair like yours.

"Tell her I was born with it. My brother and sister have curly hair too. Mor never needs to curl her hair, neither did Bestamor."

"Mor? Bestamor? Who are they?" questioned River. Grandmother gave each of the young men quizzical looks but remained patient for an answer to her question.

"Mor is mother and Bestamor is grandmother. Sorry."

More conversation transpired between the three and glances were given in his direction as the two explained Bjorn's curly headed family members. An argument arose between River and grandmother when she reached to touch one of Bjorn's unruly curls that hung behind his ear.

"Trouble?" asked Bjorn with a smile in his voice.

"She wants a curl. To help remember you."

Bjorn turned to her and said, "This one?" and she nodded her head, yes. Reaching for his knife that was on his belt, he cut the curl off and handed it to her.

Taking a small piece of leather retrieved from a basket beside her, grandmother took the curl, gently placed it on the leather scrap, rolled the scrap up and put the treasure in the basket. Reaching for Bjorn's hand, she uttered, "Memories. Good for old," and she pointed to herself. Commotion outside disrupted more conversation. The two young boys who had taken the reins of the horses to curry, feed and water them brought in the *parfleche* wrappings from behind the saddles and placed them in front of grandmother.

"Smell good," came from her as she unwrapped the first, discovering the salmon. "Mmmm!" exploded from her, louder than Bjorn would have expected from such an aged person. "Did good," she spoke. "Good friend. Good food." With that declared, she motioned for the group assembled now to leave, content to nibble on her most favorite fish, salmon.

"Need to ride," Delaware said. "Need to get back to the train by nightfall."

They saddled up and rode back down the same trail they had come. The blazing sun's position on the horizon indicated there were about three hours of daylight left.

"River, ready to trade with Pig's Eye again?" asked Delaware as they returned. "Medicines supplied for trade again? Frontier people always looking for medicine."

"So wasn't an accident that you knew how to set that bone?" suggested Bjorn.

"*Okomisan's* been teaching me since I was old enough to learn uses for plants. She'd take me with her when she went looking for roots and herbs. Made me repeat the names of each as we filled her basket."

"Train could sure use your skills. Know how to birth a baby? Leif's wife is about due."

"Have pain medicine. Birthing is woman's work," offered River, making the birthing process sound demeaning for a man.

"How much longer until we get to Carver's Cove? Must be a doctor there."

"Need to get to Fort Beauharnois on the shore of Lake Pepin, first. Right, Delaware?"

"Beauharnois? Sounds French. When were they here?"

"Fort's on a wide part of that Mississippi River which starts somewhere in the Territories. That post is the last stop before Carver's Cove," came from Delaware.

"You'll need to talk to Pig's Eye. Fur Trapper and Fire Water peddler. He'll know about the French Voyageurs," was Delaware's suggestion. Peddlers make fire water. Sell it to us and to the trappers and traders," said Delaware.

"Fire water? Like whiskey?"

"Makes us act crazy. We two don't use it," came from River. "Need to have clear heads up in the Territories. Too much danger."

The next few days and nights on the trail blended into each other. Wagon masters were used to the routine and navigated the rough trail and sudden puddles with little difficulty. Horses, oxen, wagons and people all seemed well oiled to the daily task of getting to the next destination. Stoppings were places sometimes which did not have names but did have a hut, a corral and a lean-to – areas where other trains had done the same. Each unloaded enough to make a meal and took care of personal necessities. Helped another who needed a strong arm. Those having animals along, especially the crated ones, made sure they were let out to wander, always guarded by a family member. Mundane tasks but essential.

Morning entailed securely packing everything that had been removed from the cart or wagon the night before.

Most times, the next destination was unknown, just a hope that it would bring one closer to the end of the trail.

One of those evenings Bjorn's duty was to see that each wagon master reported to the center circle and a communal fire. When all had gathered, Stone announced to the group, "Check your provisions. At Fort Beauharnois sometime tomorrow. Will stay two days so you can take care of restocking and other personal needs. Spices, raisins, sugar, candles, flour, potatoes, beans, turnips, onions, repairs. Small fort but friendly farming people. "

Tunson who was always the last in line because his was the largest wagon now yelled, "Any chance to replace harness on one of the drafts?"

"Problem is the load they pull. Too much punishment for your team. Drafts have lost weight too. Not because they haven't been fed. Because you've asked too much of them," came from the hard voiced Stone.

"Harness maker was the question," boomed Tunson, so loud that those cooking at the campfire came around to the area where the men were gathered and faced the group, wondering what was causing the argument.

"Army post! What do you think? Not always willing to service abused animals." Stone paused a little as he continued to stare at Tunson. "Tell the women that they'll be invited to tea one of the afternoons we are there. Tradition of the Commander's wife. Her way to greet newcomers."

Chapter 17

Two days in one place along a slow moving river more like a lake was like giving the women a purse full of gold to spend as frivolously as they wanted. Each wagon master's cart or wagon was positioned in a secluded area by one of the corporals whose duty it was to leave room for privacy and yet keep them within the confines of the fort's protection. The Potawatomi had just moved into this area and the Sioux were making sure their hunting lands were not infringed upon. Troops patrolled daily, making sure their fire arms were very visible to deter any conflict.

"Seen Gray Eagle yet?" questioned River when he met Delaware at the cook's wagon, ready to have Cook's evening stew. The two quickly caught four beautiful lake trout while Corporal Trace took over the duty of mustering the train wagons to their places.

"Haven't. Need to ride later tonight up to the bluffs. Most likely waiting for me to find him."

"Who's Gray Eagle?" came from Bjorn, wondering how Delaware always seemed to know someone at the next major stopping place.

"Uncle. Spent time with the Yaocomico back east when he was sent to negotiate with the government."

"Be sure to ask about the Sioux. What he knows about their gathering to the west of here," offered River. "If I continue north to see what the trade possibilities are with the Northwest Fur Traders, I'll need to know."

"You going north?" asked Bjorn with surprise in his voice.

"Being sent by our people. Northerners are always looking for cures. Not good at processing meat. Get sick easily. Careless with their tools and cause themselves wounds. Need herb poultices.

"Grandmother has many of our people preparing medicine bags to sell," revealed Delaware. "River is a good healer himself."

"Will you let me follow along? I need to get to Old Crossing. Have an uncle there. Want to see if there is free land to settle on in that area or a place close to him. Tells me it's the *land of milk and honey,*" stated Bjorn.

"Might be a land of milk and honey if you're one of those bee keepers you left behind and you have a milk cow or two. Land needs to be claimed. Sod turned and planted. Woods cleared off it. Tall prairie grass covers the open areas. Ready for that?" asked River.

"*Ja.* Used to work when I wasn't herding sheep. Spent many hours behind a horse or two and a fallow."

"Delaware says you've surprised him. Think more like one of us. Get Red. Let's see if we can find Gray Eagle. Be careful though."

"Why now?"

Coming over to Bjorn, River reached over and pulled one of the curls that dangled at the base of Bjorn's neck and free of the stocking cap he usually wore. "Make a good trophy for a spear head" which caused both Delaware and he to belly laugh. Still chuckling, River reached for the reins of his horse, grabbed the pommel, gracefully flew into the saddle, and headed out of the circle towards the sandstone cliffs farther down the river from the confines of the fort.

"How could I be so lucky? Accepted by both braves and their people. Finding a guide to the Territories and one with skills to cure the simple aches and pains I know the New World holds," thought Bjorn as he followed intently on Red behind River.

They left the stockade around the fort and came closer to the cliffs and a narrow space between the swollen river and the base of those cliffs. A swallow's screeching call floated over the water. River stopped so abruptly that Bjorn had to halt beside him in order not to rear end Scout. Looking up, River spotted Gray Eagle sitting on one of the sandstone ledges waving to him.

Dismounting, River allowed Scout to wander as he instructed Bjorn to do the same with Red. "Climb with me."

Struggling to find solid footing was a new experience for Bjorn, used to the mountainous region where he came from. There, the slippery moss that formed on the ledges could be a problem. Here, it was the loose sand and ledge areas that easily gave way to his weight. Reaching the area where the two were already talking, Bjorn seated himself to the side of River and waited.

"Going North?" came from the steel-bodied man with a head of gray hair that denoted age. A hand and arm shot out to Bjorn, who was ready to accept the traditional hand clasp and arm to elbow touch as greeting.

"Glad to have River as guide," explained Bjorn, impressed with the clear, spoken English.

"Sioux may be a problem. Not so much up north where you're going. Around here. Land keeps being claimed by others moving in. Hunting land is less and less. Government sends soldiers. Most don't respect Indian ways."

"My Uncle Olaf tells me the land is there for the taking if you work and make improvements."

"That's the problem. Some of that land is Indian land, not the governments."

"How will I know?"

"River can help. Traders know. Need to listen. Not claim so quickly." He paused and looked at the sun beginning to set. Need to get back. Long ride ahead. No moon." Greetings were done, this time as a parting and Bjorn watched as Gray Eagle scaled the shale cliff in places where Bjorn saw no foot hold possible.

Bjorn's descent back down to Red was even more treacherous. Unsure of footing and not being able to see where to place his feet burdened his journey the short distance to the base of the sandstone cliff. He found the roan, contentedly nibbling on shards of grass that grew here and there along the river's shore.

When the two returned to the post, Bjorn heard fiddle music and a harmonica playing. Five couples danced on an area that had been paved with the smooth rock he'd just scaled. The protection of the fort had a calming effect on the new arrivals. They relied on the military present to do what was needed if a threat ensued. Tired from a long day in the saddle, so many twists and turns to his plans, and his own peace that River would be his guide as he sought his dream, Bjorn took his bed roll, cleared an area of the few small pebbles visible under Cook's wagon and lay down, trying to sort in his mind all that had transpired today and its relationship to the next few months.

"Bjorn. Bjorn," came through the fog in his mind.

"Wha ?" was his sleepy reply.

"Stone needs us," explained Delaware, already dressing and picking up his bed roll.

"Now what?' asked Bjorn as he too dressed and labored with the bed roll that did not want to cooperate.

"Two horses stolen and a pig. Don't think it's Sioux. Can't be far off. Pig should give them away."

Not bothering to saddle up, both used the mane of their horses to aide in balancing them as they leaped onto their animals, urging them to move. Delaware ahead was leaning low and watching the ground for signs of the escapees. In no time, the two heard the pig, slowed their pace, slid off and tethered their horses. Moving along the edge of the trail, hunched over and in the shadow of the tall grasses, the two halted just before reaching a slight clearing. Two men and two younger youth sat around a small fire which had a chicken spitted and roasting. A bottle was being passed between the two older fellows. One downed a good portion of the liquid before passing it back to the other. "Liquor," mouthed Delaware so lowly that Bjorn strained hard to hear. "Wait. Let the liquor do its work." Wait they did and soon the two men were sound asleep as were the younger boys who had early on lost interest in the bottle passing.

"What now?" whispered Bjorn quietly.

Delaware handed Bjorn four leather ropes and one of the rags he'd used to wipe Wind down when the animal had been run hard. The rope material was thinner than the bridle ropes but long and strong enough to tie someone or something down. Pointing to the older of the two, Delaware said, "Yours," and gestured to his hands and feet. "Mine," and he pointed to the other.

"Lads?"

"Be too scared to run too far. Later." As noiselessly as he could Delaware crawled towards the younger man, stuffed his mouth with the rag, flipped him on his stomach and tied his hands and feet together. Bjorn, he noticed, was about done doing the same. The young lads continued to sleep. The pig's continual squealing served as cover for any noise the men or the two intruders made. "It's yours," came from Delaware as he pointed to the pig. "Horses mine."

Bjorn found the sack it had been carried in when the men came from the fort. Using it once again, he grabbed the animal by its tied back legs, dropped it head first in the sack, secured the sack with a piece of rope lying on the ground and hurried after Delaware who had freed the horses and was leading them back to their own mounts.

The pig, jostling on Bjorn's back as he hurried down the path, continued its shrill squeaks. Reaching the four horses, Delaware tethered one to Wind and one to Red. Bjorn handed the sack to Delaware, grabbed Red's mane and mounted. Retrieving the sac, Bjorn placed it across the haunches of Red, so that even in the sack the pig's legs were sprawled out like it would be lying somewhere. Either the warmth of Red's body or the feeling of something solid under it quieted the animal.

Delaware led the way in the darkness, void of any moon to guide them. Stone met them as they came to the gate of the post and waited for an explanation.

"Liquor. Poor farmers probably. Needing food and horses to use behind a plow," reported Delaware.

"Four. Two men and two young boys who never woke up when we tied the fathers," explained Bjorn.

"Need to see Cook. Need a couple more rags for my pack. Used the two I had to stuff their mouths."

Stone laughed. "Your horse rags?" It was the first time on the whole trip Bjorn had heard Stone laugh.

The two left Stone who was headed towards the Corporal on duty to report the return of the stock. Delaware took the two horses and tethered them alongside the others with a warning to the person on guard duty to be more attentive. Bjorn found the wagon master whose pig crate stood empty, opened the sack, lifted out the pig and returned it to its pen.

Chapter 18

Dawn was breaking on the horizon so Bjorn headed back to Cook's wagon to see if he could help him. What he found surprised him. "No food? No fire going? Cook sick? What's wrong?" wondered Bjorn, unsure what to do about his discovery.

"Tether him, Bjorn," came from Cook climbing out of his wagon and rubbing sleep from his eyes. "We join the military for breakfast today. Tradition at this post."

One of the larger wood pole longhouses served as the cook's wagon for the military. Inside, long hand hewn tables and benches ran down its center in two rows. Five company men assigned this day for kitchen duty were already carrying to the tables heaping plates of pancakes, bacon, sausage, grits of some sort, muffins, eggs done a variety of ways and steaming coffee cups. As fast as the food was set down, it disappeared. "Do they always eat this well?" asked Bjorn, amazed at what he saw happening.

"Usually they get a ration of food at each meal with little choice of its content. Because we came and are being fed, the government wants to impress us. The military assigned here is glad to see us come," he told Bjorn with a grin on his face. "Best meals they get are when visitors come. Been to the commissary?"

"Commissary?"

"Post store? Need anything?"

Bjorn thought and then said, "Don't know. Best I ask River what I need unless you can help me."

"Ask him. Don't know what he's got in his pack. Might determine what you should offer to carry or need."

Bjorn lingered longer than usual over the meal. He was not a good early morning eater. It wasn't the pattern he lived when in the mountains. There he checked the herd first, rounded those lambs that had strayed at night, and fed his dogs. Then, he took care of himself by making a simple mush or ate bread and cheese if he had any left from his brother Erik's visit. The coffee pot sat on the side of the fire pit that smoldered all day long near his hut on the mountainside. The first cups were good but the longer the brewed coffee seethed in the fire, the stronger it got. No matter what, Bjorn had to have his coffee. When it tasted this good, especially after drinking trail coffee made from so many different tasting waters, it was hard to leave the table.

Seeing River sitting alone across the room on the other side of the long hall filled with tables empty of men and food, Bjorn decided to find out whether he needed to go to the commissary or not. "Good food," complimented River when Bjorn sat down across from him. "Not good company."

"Want me to leave?" asked Bjorn with a disturbed look on his face, wondering what he had done to make River unhappy with him.

"Not you. Rest left just as I sat down to eat. Don't like Indians, I'd guess."

"Happen often?" spoke Bjorn, curious to know what might be in store as the two journeyed north.

"Often enough. Depends whether what I have, what I can do, or what I might know is needed."

"People are the same all over. I left because I had no money. My father had less. Working on the *gard* in the Nordic mountains for Israelson, herding his spring lambs was not hard work. No future. No family possibilities.

Couldn't support one. A common laborer, the lowest of the low."

"Miss home?"

"*Ja*, miss my Mor, Far, brother Erik and Anna, my little sister. Don't miss the loneliness of the *stol* where I stayed with the sheep for weeks on end, seeing no one, only a wolf or two."

"Looks like we're being summoned," came from River, pointing to the far door where Stone stood beckoning.

"Want to stop at Pig's Eye's tavern. Not sure it is wise. Don't know what this train of people would do if the place is full of riff raff," said Stone to the two when they came close enough to hear.

"All three of us going? Must be some real riff raff you're worried about if we all need to go," commented River, used to only one being sent for such a duty.

"Take Bjorn here and go. He needs the experience. You might need his white skin," bantered Stone, appearing to be in one of his better moods.

"Skin or hair?" came from River.

"I'd like to keep both my skin and hair if you two don't mind," returned Bjorn.

All three left the long building that served as a kitchen for the men at the post, Stone went to take care of other duties and Bjorn and River went to find Cook and Delaware to tell each that they had been sent out on a mission.

"Where'll we find this Pig's Eye person?" asked Bjorn, wanting to be a little knowledgeable.

"There's a cave close to a small community forming and calling themselves Carver's Cove. Pierre must have discovered it on one of his return trips to sell his furs that he bought or traded for with the trappers and Indians in the Northwest Territory. The cave has a spring inside which provides a steady water supply."

"Must be in one of the sandstone banks somewhere? Doesn't seem like caves in these banks would be too safe, especially if there's a stream flowing to wash away part of the walls."

"Caves differ. Walls in this one are granite, I think, or at least a hard rock."

"So, you've been there before? Know him?"

"Traded with him. He likes the medicine. Sells easily in the Territory. Stayed with him a time or two when the weather was so stormy I couldn't travel back to my people," came from River in a reflective voice. "He lost an eye somehow, not sure what happened. Wears a patch. Helps to pick him out in a dark inn," said River.

"What do we do when we get to where this cave is?"

"Need to find it first. Haven't been there in a while. Probably try and trade some of the medicine in my *parfleche*. If he takes it all, I'll have to go back and visit grandmother to replace the stash. It'll delay us some time. You all right with that?"

"Have to be. Don't want to travel north without you. Can't risk my greenness stopping me from finding my uncle. Need you a lot more than you need me."

Chapter 19

    A day's riding and another half searching the cliffs and riverbank kept the two occupied, and somewhat concerned that the train would get to wherever Pig's Eye was camped before they did. River admitted to being disoriented, an unusual situation for him. "Came here during a storm and arrived at night the last time. Everything is always different at night." Looking at the area and the cliffs along the bank of the river ahead, he sorted landmarks in his mind and finally decided that the furthest outcropping visible from this point was probably where they needed to go.

    Rounding the bend of the river, Bjorn was surprised to see a small inn inside a substantial corral.

"That's it. Let's hope he's there."

"And if he isn't?"

"We use his place like others do. Doesn't care as long as it is left the way it's found. The cave's up behind that outcropping." Setting Scout into a gentle lope, he continued, "Not as hard as you think – leaving his place as is. Inn is small. Has a big fire pit inside. See the chimney? No table or chairs. Only sturdy logs to sit on around the fire pit. No beds. Sleep on the floor if you want to join what crawls."

A small statured man, dressed in frontier leggings and a leather, fringed jacket, came out and stood in the doorway as the two approached. "Heard you coming." Staring with the one eye, he said, "River, is that you? Must be a wagon train coming. Stone as ornery as ever?"

"Stone's train of forty wagons should be here tomorrow, noon. Were fifty. Lost a few along the way."

"Stone order them out?"

"No, group is inexperienced but cooperative. Bee keepers stayed in Medina. One tried a new area to cross the river. Wagon fell in a hole so he lost everything. Another liked the land and dropped out. Typical losses like that."

"Who's he?" asked Pig's Eye, with some skepticism in his voice. "If he didn't have a beard, I'd think you found a woman. Look at those curls!"

Ignoring the hair comments, Bjorn slid off Red, extended his hand and said, "I'm Bjorn. Looking to find land in the Territories around Old Crossing. Know of any available?"

"Pierre Parrant's the name but most call me Pig's Eye 'cause of the patch." He reached for Bjorn's hand to shake and added, "Haven't been to Old Crossing in a while. Why that place?"

"Uncle there or at least I think so if nothing has happened to him."

"Let me think on it." Shifting his weight and moving from the door frame, he continued, "Water your horses and tether them there," pointing to a railing made for that purpose. "I'll see if the stew in the pot is ready. Caught a rabbit. Come in when you done. Coffee's on. We'll talk if the pot needs more time to simmer."

Once inside, the two sat on logs that were around the fire pit. The small smoldering fire served as a stove of sorts for cooking and heat at night. Taking a cup of coffee handed to him by Pig's Eye, Bjorn asked, "Who do you trade with?"

"River for one. His medicine bags sell out up in the Territories where there isn't a doctor.

"Any Companies?" came from Bjorn in a curious voice.

"One I've always traded with, McKenzie and Chouteau. Why you ask, son?"

"Heard there were two up in the Territories Don't think those are the names I've heard," said Bjorn as he removed his stocking cap and tried to shake his curls free from the flattening the cap caused.

"Hudson Bay or the Northwest Company the names you've heard?"

"*Ja*. Northwest is the one I've heard."

"Good traders. Fair."

"The Bay traders aren't?"

"Not that so much. Northwest Company traders bring their furs and other items to Carver's Cove and the river here," motioned Pig's Eye, indicating the flowing water just outside his door. "The Bay skins get sent north and up into the lakes and Europe some way, I guess." Pig's Eye refilled the coffee cups, stirred the stew and tasted it to see if it was ready but sat down again. "Planning on trapping?"

"*Nei*, never done much of that. Need to see what the land is like. Decide then what I'll do. Plant. Raise a herd of sheep. Don't know . . . " came from Bjorn as he realized that his dream of the free land didn't include a plan for it.

"Sheep? Might have trouble raising them," River commented.

"Why's that?"

"Anyone with any large animal herd lets them graze freely. Few fences. Most hate sheep. Don't know why," said River.

"Sheep strip the land if you don't move them from place to place. Don't suppose they are too available to buy as stock either, then," offered Bjorn with concern.

"You'd have to buy them in Carver's Cove or Sauk River trading post and herd them back to your place," decided Pig's Eye.

"Sauk River?"

"A larger community that's gathered where the Mississippi goes north and the Sauk River goes west. People follow the river north on one trail or turn west on the other trail to go up to Old Crossing, Pembina and Fort Gary," shared Pig's Eye.

"We'll be heading west. Want to get to Otter Tail. Promised trappers there that I'd bring supplies next time out."

"That anywhere close to Old Crossing?" asked Bjorn, interested in the lay of the land.

"Crossing's north and a little to the west of there, not far," said River.

Rising and reaching for what looked to be three large spoon-shaped, wooden carved bowls with handles, Pig's Eye took the ladle that was in the stew pot and filled each, handing one to River and to Bjorn. Filling his own, he sat back on his stool and blew on the steaming contents. Bjorn waited and was surprised when he saw River take his knife from the sheath along his beltline and use it to spear a piece of the meat out of the steam. Deciding spoons were not going to be offered, Bjorn did the same, amazed how good the rabbit stew tasted. Meat was tender and had a flavor unfamiliar to Bjorn. What couldn't be speared with success, the three used two fingers to scoop the contents. Each slurped the dregs from the bowl, not wanting to waste food.

"Better turn in. Need help in the morning. See what fish are willing to be supper. What driftwood is dry enough to fuel the fire for the big pot. Tinder to start it." After laying out the early morning plans, Pig's Eye took the empty pot and the three spoon bowls along with the pot's ladle and headed out to the river to wash them. "Good," he thought. "Clear sky." Rain meant he'd have to bring the big pot into the inn and build a bigger fire, causing lots of smoke that the chimney wouldn't handle.   Stone paid ten cents per person for the meal when anyone cooked for the wagon train at a stop. Good money this time of year. He needed all he could accumulate so he could buy the medicine stash River had wrapped in that animal skin behind his saddle.   River used his cash, Pig's Eye knew, to buy ammunition and guns for his tribe. If buying the medicine left him flat, he'd just have to sell more liquor.

Bjorn was the first to wake, used to rising early to tend the sheep and recently to swab the deck of the schooner he'd come over on to the New World. He gathered kindling first. Bits of dried grass washed up on shore were easy to find. Smaller twigs were scattered with the grass. Bjorn used the front of his shirt as an apron to hold what he was gathering. Looking around, he saw a blackened area circled by stones that he decided must be the outside fire pit. "Two loads should be enough kindling," decided Bjorn as he looked at the pile. "Wood. Hmmm. Don't see a stack," he thought as he scanned the open space. Seeing what looked like a tree of some sort farther down the beach, Bjorn took the hatchet hanging beside the doorway and headed for it. The dry tree, now more like driftwood, easily cut into pieces that he could carry. He spent the rest of the early daylight hours doing so, first building stacked tree cuttings over the kindling and then piling the rest close at hand to feed the flames when more fuel was needed for the fire.

"Bjorn," hailed River, slowly loping up to the pit. "Let me hand this doe to you. She's field dressed. Need to skin her and spit her. Shouldn't need that stew pot tonight."

The two worked quickly, carefully removing the skin. Once freed, River took it to Pig's Eye who'd just finished assembling the apparatus he used for stretching and drying fur. Leaving the carcass to the two men to position over the fire on the iron attachments he'd handed them, Pig's Eye went to scrape the skin and ready it for drying.

"Good timing," offered Bjorn, hearing the rumbling and squeaking of the oxcart and wagon wheels. "Wonder if frogs come out of the river at night here. Sounds like some of the wagon masters forgot to grease the wheels."

"Stone won't worry so this time. We're too close to the end of the trail. Just need to get them to Carter's Cove. Means one more stop between here and the Cove," and he saw Bjorn's face light up. "Glad to be done scouting soon?"

"*Nei*, have enjoyed that really. Learned a lot too. *Tukk*. Just anxious to get to the Territory and see how much Olaf lied about that *land of milk and honey*," Bjorn shared, sure that the road ahead would not be easy. "Where'd you find the doe?"

"Saw her out of the corner of my eye back a ways on the trail. Saw tracks to the river that I knew were deer. She was watering and didn't see me draw my arrow. Heard another run. Didn't see it. Didn't care. Needed only this one."

Stopping the scraping and washing his hands, Pig's Eye went into the Inn and shortly came out with a huge covered pot in one hand and a sack of flour in the other. Looking at Born, he said, "Ever used a rock as an oven to make bread?"

Taking the two items from Pig's Eye, Bjorn chuckled, "I have lots of times up in the mountain. That's all I often had – bread I'd made and cheese from the *stol*."

"*Stol*?" questioned Pit's Eye who turned back from his returning to the inn. "The farm had a *stol*?"

"*Ja*. More than one. Unless I saw something to hit with my sling shot and cook like this over a spit, I ate bread I made and cheese." Bjorn waited, expecting Pig's Eye to bring him a container for mixing and he did. The hollowed out log that served as a trencher or bowl had seen other mixings. Bjorn took the sack of corn meal down to the river bank and mixed enough meal and water to make a dough for seven good sized loaves. Once mixed to his liking, Bjorn returned to the fire pit and saw seven smaller plankings. Using these plankings, he broke the mixture in seven sections, formed each into a loaf and set them close to the fire so the dough could rise. Seven rocks were already placed near the fire's edge and Bjorn knew that they were his baking stones.

Pig's Eye greeted every wagon master as they entered the encircled area where the inn was situated. Each master kept his place in line and began the process of parking. First, the animals were cared for. Seeing no hay stack was visible, grass stashed under the wagon or cart came out. A stop down the road the next day would be used to replace the supply.

Bjorn watched the women who were delighted to see the doe roasting. Each quickly found their frying pan, took potatoes, other vegetables and a little lard from their supply they'd replenished at the fort and came to the edge of the fire. The roasted vegetables made a nice addition to the venison they knew would be shared for the evening meal.

River gathered the younger children who now had buckets in hand and escorted them to the bank of the river, cautioning them to be careful of the fast flowing stream. No sooner had the warning been made than one girl tripped as she tangled in the skirt of her dress. Screams were heard as she bobbed her way down river with the current. Stripping off his shirt, leggings and moccasins, River ran into the river and then dove in the direction of the girl whose head was no longer visible. Wagon members gathered and began to pray. Neither head was visible. A murmur rumbled through the gathering crowd, concerned not only for the girl but for River. Suddenly, River emerged from the water carrying the limp girl in his arms. He placed her on the bank and began to try and revive her. As the mother reached her, the girl moved under the straddling brave. Turning her over and seating her on his lap, River heard rasping breaths come from her.

"Mama?"

"I'm here," and the mother took her in her arms.

River quickly turned away from the crowd, returned to the river's edge and dove back into the water. Swimming up stream of the flowing water was taxing but his strong strokes made headway quickly to where his clothes lay. His muscular body covered only in his breechcloth glistened with rivulets that flowed off him when he emerged from the river to redress.

"How'd you find her?" asked Bjorn who'd come down to the river to be close to the other children and watched the process, as concerned for River as he was for the girl.

"Snagged on a tree below the water. Wouldn't have saved her if she hadn't. Water too fast, faster than I could get to her."

"Master of talents," said Bjorn as he hugged the man he'd grown to admire for more than one reason.

"Worried about the rest when I went in after her. Some little ones there that could hardly hold the bucket let alone carry it full."

"Rest backed away. Some ran back without filling their bucket. Older ones helped the younger ones finally."

"Why I got my name," explained River. "Born by a river. Chief named me." Rest of the story got left untold as the father of the girl came towards him.

"How can I pay you? Only child. Scared of water. What happened?"

"Tripped on the skirt of her dress. Took her off balance. She snagged on a tree limb below the water or I don't think I could have caught up to her."

"Pay?" came from the hard faced, calloused hands that were extended towards River.

"None expected. Help one of mine if you have the chance wherever you settle. We'll all be in trouble if we don't learn to get along." River reached for the extended hand and clasped it as he stepped forward to complete the familiar greeting of hand to upper arm. Seeing Stone near the cook's wagon, he excused himself and walked in that direction.

Pig's Eye, full of surprises, came out of the inn with a fiddle in his hand and joined the group gathered around the fire pit, each enjoying the venison portions that had been added to their frying pans. "Need a little music after the scare today," he offered. "Not the best fiddle player you'll ever hear. Squeak like your wheels once in a while."

"Don't care," came from a sunburned faced woman sitting by her two children. "Fought that ox all day. Stubborn animal. Need something to make me forget my aches."

"Stone wants us," came from Delaware this time just as the fiddler began to play. Bjorn knew there were new duties ahead of him and followed beside as Delaware continued talking. "Stone's wondering how many other wagon trains are on the road between here and Carver's Cove. Needs to be sure of a safe spot for the last night out."

"Trouble?" asked Bjorn, not sure what Delaware meant about a safe spot.

"First night out and the last night out can always be trouble. Thieves. Steal livestock. Barrels that are not protected. Don't really care what's in them. Sell what they find. Hope you got a good night's sleep last night."

"Not really. Pig snored. Woke me more than once. Finally gave up, got up and gathered wood for the pit."

"No sleep tonight, either," assured Delaware. "This time the three of us will ride."

"Guess I'll earn my pay tonight," thought Bjorn. "Wonder what I'll be looking for and where."

"Men," came from Stone who had a coffee cup in his hand and was leaning against Cook's wagon. "You two know what to do" and he pointed to Delaware and River. "Tell him what he needs to do. Make it easy for him. Remember he's green."

"That word again! Will it ever leave me?" wondered Bjorn, but he didn't say anything.

"Need to find a spot. You know. Won't start a fire. Just camp. Women won't be happy to hear they can't have fire. Don't want to advertise any more than we have to."

"Ten miles or so do?" asked Delaware, trying to understand how far they needed to ride before they started looking for a spot.

"Should do. I'll have one or two of the wagon masters ride behind, protecting our backs. The women will drive their rigs."

"That serious?" came from River, surprised that the train needed lookouts in back.

"Sioux are kicking up a fuss," offered Delaware. "Found out last night when Otter signaled for me to meet him. Saw me from the bluffs and wanted to warn me."

"What was that Ojibwa doing down this far?" said River. "He's an Old Crossing friend."

"Why he signaled," and the rest of the reasons for the visit were not shared as Stone motioned for the three to be on the trail.

Chapter 20

"You lead, Bjorn. See anything strange, pull on that curl behind your right or left ear. Keep moving. I'll know which way to look that way," instructed River. "Delaware, keep an eye on the ground. I'll keep an eye above us."

Horses moved along the trail as though tethered together in a straight line, so comfortable were they with each other. Riders looked relaxed but were far from that as they navigated the bumps and grinds of the wheel tracks left by oxcarts, wagons, horses and oxen. Birds along the shore of the Mississippi scattered when the trio neared. A flash of light caught Bjorn's eye through the leaves of one of the few scattered bushes along the trail so he scratched at the curl behind his left ear but moved on ahead as though nothing were amiss. Once alongside the sighting, Bjorn leaned over Red, head down, and scratched at the roan's mane too but at the same time tried to look into the brush. Nothing was visible to him and he continued on like he'd been told. A few steps ahead Bjorn heard a yelp and turned back to see River astride a small child no more than six or seven, now whimpering. Delaware, off his horse and already up on higher ground, scanned the area for more of the child's family. Nothing.

"Where's you mother?" questioned River, helping the child to stand in front of him. No answer came.

Bjorn dismounted and knelt on his one knee so he could be at eye level with the child he thought must be about seven years old and said, "What happened? Lost? Pony run off?"

"Left. Too many children. Can't feed us. Dad said he'd come back and get me. Fell asleep." The whimpering started again. "Two nights here. Never came back."

"Which way were you headed?" asked River.

"That way" and the child pointed to the trail in front of them heading north.

"What do we do?" asked Bjorn. "Keep him with us?"

"I'll take him back to the train. He can help Cook unless someone else will have him. Not the first time we've found someone out on the trail alone. Take it slow. I'll catch up with you later today. Trouble – drop those small orange dyed leather pieces, Delaware. I'll be watching."

Lifting the wide eyed child unto the horse, River set his mount at a gallop, trying not to tax the animal too much, knowing he'd have to keep him fresh for the return.

"Left? Seems impossible someone would just leave their child out here."

"Women have been left too," stated Delaware. "Keep an eye," and he rode ahead wondering what to do if they did find the family camping ahead.

Shadows from the few trees along the trail moved across it as the sun began its descent. Rounding a corner where the river divided, a remnant of what had been someone's campsite came into view. Delaware dismounted, took a stick and dug into the center of the fire pit, placed his hand over the digging and said, "Someone stayed here last night. Tether your horse. We'll wait on that ledge. Need to give River time to get back to us," came from him as he pointed to a shale overhang. "Sleep while you can. I'm going to scout around."

Red made his way to the river bank, leaned and drank. Adjusting the blanket and saddle, Bjorn led the roan back to the camp site, found a stake he could use for tethering and anchored Red near a small growth of green grass that the horse had already discovered. Reaching the ledge looked impossible until he spotted two slabs a little farther down about at the height where he could scramble up each and finally get to the ledge. He skittered a little as he maneuvered his way up but finally reached the smooth area just above his horse. Reaching in his pouch at his waist, Bjorn removed a small piece of jerky, deciding this would be tonight's supper. Leaning against the back of the overhang, Bjorn thought again about the young lad. Sleep came in spurts between anger at the family, concern for the boy, and a greater concern for River who still hadn't returned.

Waking once, the night shadows made him skittish. He looked at Red and realized the horse was asleep if horses slept while standing. The fear he'd felt left, knowing that an animal's sense of danger was far greater than man. When Delaware's hand came to rest on his shoulder, Bjorn jumped and grabbed for his knife in its leather case at his side.

"Relax. Thought you heard me. No River yet, ha? Should be here soon, I'd think. If his horse isn't too winded, we'll continue our ride."

"Didn't hear you. Thought you . . . " and this time Bjorn didn't finish as the two heard hoof beats coming down the trail opposite where River should be coming.

Flattening their bodies as far back on the ledge as they could and yet see the trail, the two waited to see who was approaching. Getting to the campsite but not yet seeing the two horses, the youth of about fourteen called, "Karl. Karl. Where are you? Going to take you back to the fort. I'm coming too. Karl. Karl. Dammit! Come out of hiding. I'm not going to hurt . . ." and then he stopped, seeing the two tethered horses.

Delaware did not give the young man time to think. He dropped down in front of the horse that neighed with surprise, and held the reins so it could not run.

"Where you got my brother?" asked the rider. "Scalped him?"

"Brother's safe. Why do you ask?"

"Where's the other one? Or are you riding two horses?" came from the straight backed boy soon to be a man.

"Asked why you want to know," questioned Delaware, releasing the hold on the horse, hoping that would loosen the boy's mouth as well.

"Ran away. Tired of not having anything to eat unless we catch something. Dad's a dreamer. Mom's worn out. Going to find Karl and get back to the fort. We'll find work there, cleaning stalls or something for the military." The boy stopped when he saw River ride into the clearing. "Who's he? 'Nother Indian. He do the scalping?"

Bjorn had heard enough from this young man, leaped over the edge and grabbed him by the collar hard enough to dismount him. "Mind your manners, young man, if you've learned any. Your brother's safe. River here took him back to the wagon train we are a part of. I'm sure he's feasting on something Cook made for supper. No one has scalped anyone. River and Delaware are my friends. I'd trust them with my life. I'm Bjorn. What's your name?"

"Burt. Sorry. Scared I'd lost him. Only one who cares about him. Rest of the family turned their backs on him. Nine of us. One every other year until mom kicked dad out of bed seven years ago and has made him sleep on the floor or ground ever since."

"When's the last you ate?" asked Delaware.

"Two nights ago when I rode ahead and caught some fish. Cleaned them too."

"Here, chew slowly," and he handed the young lad a good sized piece of jerky. "How far ahead is the rest of the family?"

"About a mile, I'd guess. They took the right trail."

"That means we'd better take the left one. Good. It's the easier of the two for the oxen. We'll leave markings for Stone when we get there. Most likely the noise of the train will scare your folks enough so that they won't move until our train has passed."

"My brother?"

"He's with the train, riding with Cook who's driving the food wagon. We need to ride out and scout the rest of the trail. Horse looks pretty good. You willing to help scout?" came from Delaware, trying to ease the mind of the young lad in front of him.

"Sure. Been doing that all along. That's why I have a horse. Rest are in the wagon or walking."

Chapter 21

Assured that Karl was safe and fed, Burt was to go first down the trail ahead that led to Carver's Cove. Bjorn would follow him at a distance. "Keep your eyes and ears open. Traders, trappers, thieves, unfriendly Indians. Can you make a bird sound?"

"How 'bout a loon?"

"Good enough. See anything. Call like a loon. I'll stop and see what comes out of the woods or grass," offered Bjorn.

"We'll be close enough to hear that gun. Shoot in the air." We'll be riding the ridges as much as we can. Need to find a place no more than two hours from here," decided River. "Stone wants to cover about ten miles today, remember?"

Delaware went to the left towards the river and River found an opening in the brush where a deer's watering trail led back into the woods and up the rise. Bjorn waited to give Burt time to lead out and then followed him close enough so he still could see him once in a while but far enough back so an intruder wouldn't suspect the two were together. Riding the trail was uneventful but a peaceful interlude in a long, tedious journey to get this far. Delaware came back with news that a spot River found just off the trail up ahead would do. Close enough to the river to water the stock. An open area to circle up and yet not be right up against the tree line. Bjorn rode ahead to tell Burt and found he had two pheasants hanging from his pommel.

"Surprise for Cook. Bet it isn't everyday he has a pheasant for the cooking pot."

"Didn't hear a shot," came from Bjorn.

"Didn't need to. Trusty slingshot works best. No noise. Doesn't scare other birds."

"Nice looking birds. Turn around. River found a place to camp. We don't need to scout ahead farther," said Bjorn. "Train shouldn't be too far back. Brother'll be surprised to see you."

The open tall grassy slopes along the trail grew so tall it hid the river from view at times. Reaching the rise of the hill, both saw the other two not far away. A small fire welcomed them as they turned towards the river off the trail.

Riding up to the evening's camping area, both took time and led their horses to the river to drink, got their own water jars filled and staked the trusty mounts near the other two horses already content with the lush grass.

Bjorn walked up to the fire and asked, "Need me to do anything for you?"

"Not 'til the train comes. Hear them so it shouldn't be too long," came from Delaware.

"No other fires, right?" asked Bjorn.

"Right. Need as little smoke as possible. Less we make our whereabouts known the better. This'll be Cook's fire and for anyone who needs it. They were told it would be a cold supper tonight."

"Possible for me to roast these before the train comes?" asked Burt as he joined the group.

"Let's do them right now. Don't want to tempt others to go hunting," decided Delaware.

In no time, Burt had the pheasant's, skinned, and innards out. River's quick trek to some brush growing by the river produced two sturdy y branches and a straight pole. Burt took them, put the two pheasants on the straight pole and placed them across the y's that River'd stood over one end of the fire pit. "We'll snack on one and give the other to Cook. Sound good?"

"Who's the train's head master?" Burt wanted to know. "How about him?"

"Cook'll figure out a way so the two of them share," said Delaware. "Probably keeping a pot of rice or mush warm from this morning in his small iron barrel he fills with hot rocks before we head down the trail."

The train's circling in to place worked like a well-oiled machine. Only difference this time from some other circles was that they were closer together, forming a fence – back ends of the wagons and carts facing out and hitching poles in to the center. The animals were loosened from their harness and any sheep or cows roamed free inside the ring. It was noisy and Bjorn wondered what difference their noise made or a larger fire would make. "Have to be deaf not to hear this ruckus," he thought, but he wasn't the head wagon master. He'd learned long ago in the Old Country to keep his mouth shut and take orders. Kept him out of trouble.

Stone stepped to the fire once all had positioned themselves and spoke in a loud voice. "Last camp for some of you. We'll reach Carver's Cove about noon tomorrow. Use the small fire here by the cook's wagon if you need to heat anything. Better if you don't. Cook has coffee. Welcome to share. No lanterns or candles after dark," instructed Stone to all gathered. Unload as little as possible. Men, sleep under your wagons or carts with a gun handy. Just a precaution. Never know what's out there, man or coyote or both. We'll leave an hour after sunup in the morning."

Chapter 22

The caravan went back to its tasks and Stone watched as Burt bear hugged Cook and handed him a piece of meat he'd kept warm near the fire. "Families. I've seen all kinds on these crossings. Most good. Some so bad, like the one these two are from," thought Stone, leaning against Cook's wagon and watching the movement of the train's people as they settled for the night. "Who'd leave one like Karl? Young. Skinny from lack of food. A boy! Extra strong arms in time. And what do I do with the two of them? Can't keep them with me." He didn't have long to wonder. Leif Larson, one of the Norse men who'd brought Bjorn to him, asking to work his way here, came to him with a cup in hand.

"Time to talk to me?"

"What's on your mind, Leif?"

"Wife and I talk. Two boys, Karl and the older one, what's his name?"

"You mean Burt?"

"*Ja*. We talk. We have only a girl. Wife can't have more. Wanted a boy. Lord thought differently. We'd take the two. Raise them as ours. Make sure they get half of what's left when we – ah – leave earth. Need strong arms to plow and plant."

"You don't know anything about the two."

"Know what the young one does. Works hard for Cook. Bjorn says older has good – sense – I think word is."

"Stay here. I'll find them. They must decide. I can't." It wasn't long and Stone came back with the two boys, curious to know why he'd come for them.

"Karl, Burt. This is Leif Larson. He, his wife and his daughter are going farther north after we get to Carter's Cove, up one of the ox cart trails."

Both boys extended their hands to shake Leif's and said hello to him.

Leif looked at both of them. "Once we get to the Cove, what'll you do?"

"Not sure," came from Burt. "Hope we can stay with Stone and his trains."

"Not a good life for the two of you," stated Stone. "Need to find a place to live if you're not going to find your family."

"We have only a daughter. Love her but wanted son. Wife and I want to take you with us to this New Territory. We will claim a few acres of land. You be our sons. Work be hard clearing land. Come with us. Make sure you have food and clothes."

"You"ll be our mom and dad?" said Karl with amazement in his voice.

"Ja. We would. Rena is your age, I think Karl. Helps as much as she can."

"Could Karl and I talk about this?" offered Burt, but his face gave way his feelings as it beamed with delight.

"Ja. After you talk, come to our wagon. Meet Helga and Rena. We wait" and he turned and walked back to his spot.

Stone left the two boys, allowing them to make their choice, grateful the decision was not left to him. "Let's go. He's good to his horses. He'll be good to us – better than dad ever was," said Karl.

"Means we go way up in that new land. Means we'll probably never see mom and the rest again. Ready for that?"

"Mom's the only one I'll miss."

"Get your things if you have anything back in the cook's wagon. Tell Cook you'll help him like you have 'till we get to Carver's Cove. Meet me at Larson's wagon. I'll find Stone and let him know."

Walking to where Stone stood leaning against a tree, drinking his refilled cup of coffee, Burt stopped in front of him, shook his hand and said, "Thanks for letting us make the decision. We'll go with him. Can't be any worse life than we've been living, at least he's promised food and clothes. Maybe he'll get me new shoes. I've grown out of these so I cut room for the toes to stick out."

"You're sure? Probably won't see your family again."

"Mom's the only one we'll miss. Told Karl to get his things out of Cook's wagon if he had anything. We'll move tonight. How can I thank you?"

"You've done enough. That pheasant was a sampling of how you've helped. Pretty good scout, I hear. They'll be good to you. Good people. Can tell by the way they treat their horse and animals. Ever milked a cow?"

"No, but I'll learn." Shaking Stone's hand and giving him a bear hug which flustered Stone, unused to displayed affection, Burt walked to meet Karl and the two made their way to the Larson wagon.

Chapter 23

The sun's peeking over the horizon across the river came early for all. Sleepy heads, especially children, rubbed eyes and scrambled into clothes. Shoes were left in the wagon, saved for times when the trail was rocky and full of burrs.

"Pull out," ordered Stone as he watched Delaware lead the people and the first cart in line.

Burt atop his horse stationed himself so he could watch the small herds of animals gather to their owners. Any reluctant critters were corralled by him and convinced to stay with their kind.

Bjorn positioned himself on the outside of the ring, making sure that the wagons and animals stayed in a reasonable line one after the other. River was up in the bluffs beyond the tall grass that separated the train and trail from the bluffs or hills, Bjorn wasn't sure what those humps were. He knew for sure they were not mountains. Once the last wagon was in line, Burt came back to ride tail with Bjorn. Stone's warning rang in their ears. "When anyone sees a glimpse of the Cove, the drivers will break line. Can't have that. Keep them in line or we'll have people and animals trampled."

"Have a good night?" asked Bjorn of Burt riding beside him.

"Slept under the wagon like always. Karl too. Cold pancakes this morning. Good."

"He's a hard sounding man with Nordic ways. Soft on the inside. You'll work hard but you'll be sons to him. You got lucky, just like I did."

"You, lucky?"

"*Ja*. Worked my way over here on a schooner. Knew nothing about ocean sailing. Worked my way here as a scout. Knew little about scouting. Delaware's been a good teacher.'

"What'll you do when we reach the Cove?"

"Go north like you. Have an uncle I want to find at Old Crossing. River's agreed to guide me. Lucky again."

"Feel bad I accused them of scalping Karl. I was frantic. Didn't want him harmed. Darned near punched dad. Decided to leave instead." Both rode in silence, waiting for the first sighting of the Cove.

"Will I see you again? I think Leif is going north too."

"Don't know. Depends upon which trail he takes. Depends upon if he follows the Mississippi or goes more west through the open prairie and . . ." and the easy conversation stopped as Tunson, last in line with his wagon and horses stopped short.

"Trouble?" asked Bjorn, riding up beside.

"No. Don't want to circle. Want to be free to join wherever or to go to an Inn. Talked to Stone last night. Said I could just pull out of line and wait. Paid him too for the extra feed for the horses he found at one of the stops. Didn't want to make the same mistake as I did before and make a run for it. Grown to respect Stone too much to do that."

"I'll leave you here then. Good luck," came from Bjorn as he shook Tunson's hand.

Chapter 24

The hurrying to reach the section of the Cove and what was set aside as Stone's Landing along the river at the South edge of the community went smoothly. Those in the front of the line used their switches to make the oxen go faster. The few who'd walked the whole way stepped aside to allow the carts and wagons room on the trail.

The caravan circled as it always had but each positioned the wagon or cart on a well-worn designated spot by a hitching post and a small fire pit. Stone told the wagon masters they could stay on that spot a week if they wanted, long enough to decide what their next trail or permanent place would be. Cook took his wagon to a more secluded spot still in the circle but next to a small thatched hut with a lean-to where another horse was visible. He climbed down and smiled, knowing inside was a rope bed to sleep in, not the hard ground or wagon bed of the past weeks on the trail.

The camp buzzed with activity. Those who walked here on the trail chose one of the camp sites where a crude tent stood, hoping it would keep them dry if rain came. A few of the wagon masters did the same but most opened the hides that covered the belongings enough to find pots and tinware, flour and other staples to make and serve meals around the pit that was theirs. A small stack of wood and kindling stood close to each pit. The wife, if the wagon master had one, started a small fire so it would be smoldering when needed.

Watching the activity and not wanting to be a burden for Cook, Bjorn dismounted, tied Red to a hitching post, leaned on a small tree that was a part of this spot and waited, unsure what he was to do now. Looking to the west and up the bluff, he saw River coming down a trail, hidden at times and open to view at others. Knowing it'd take him time to come down to the camp site, Bjorn went to the spot where the lady was who he had helped with her wheel and sore footed ox. "End of the trail. I'll be leaving soon. Need any manpower before I go?"

"Not manpower. Advice on what I do next would be good," came from the concerned face.

"Not sure what I'm going to be doing so I don't know how I can advise you," chuckled Bjorn, hoping to ease her mind. "Continuing with the next train north or west?"

"Don't know. Need to go into the community and see if there is work. Don't know what kind of work I'm looking for is the problem. If I stay, I'll need to find a place. So many decisions. Makes me nervous."

"Talk to Cook. Looks like he's been here more than once since he has that hut there which must be home when he's not on the trail. Maybe he'll have some suggestions."

"Good idea. Once again you are a help and I have little to offer you in return. Oh, I do have one thing. When's the last time you had any gingerbread?"

"Since I left the Old Country. Mom made it all the time."

Going to her wagon, she reached into a tin box and removed a loaf wrapped in linen. Breaking it in half, she said, "Here. Enjoy. Hope the bread doesn't make you too homesick. " The conversation stopped as River rode up to them.

"Trouble?" came from River with concern on his face.

"Not this time. Only questions I have no answers for. Will talk to Cook as Bjorn suggests. Need to decide what to do next, go north or west or stay here."

"We'll be leaving as soon as Bjorn is ready. I can't stay here unless I stay in the cave up there. Delaware and I are not sure we are always welcome there either. Used to be our tribe's burial cave. The Sioux have come. Most of our people are across the river on the east there now. Sioux wanted to talk to Delaware and me. Wanted to know about our scouting. We told them little so they don't start their warring. Delaware'll stay with Cook. He'll come back to camp here late at night and leave early in the morning until Stone leaves again to go east. Think I'd better get your curls on the road north. Wouldn't want any to be decorations on one of the Sioux's war clubs," chided River, unsure of how much what he said of the curls was truth.

"Need a haircut?" came from the woman, leaning on her cart.

"Could use one. Hasn't been cut since I left the Old Country. Tired of this long tail that hangs."

"Here. Sit on the log and I'll get my scissors. Least I can do if you trust me."

"Hair grows back. Be good to have a lighter feeling head when the temperature gets warmer."

"Save a curl or two for Delaware and me. We'll trade them," offered River. "Might save our hides down the road. Need to see Stone. When you're done, come and find me."

Feeling light headed from the haircut, Bjorn took the curls she gave him, now wrapped in a linen cloth, thanked her, wished her well and headed to Cook's hut where he saw Stone and River talking. "Present for you," came from Bjorn as he handed over the linen bundle. "Need to share with Delaware. I don't want to part with more."

"Told Stone here we'd be leaving shortly. Delaware already knows and will meet us up a ways along the trail."

"I'll miss you. Still got some greenness in you. Always did more than asked. Aren't many like that anymore. Hope you find Olaf, isn't that his name?" said Stone.

"River's been to Old Crossing. If he's alive, we'll find him, I'm sure. Thanks isn't hardly enough for all you've done for me. You've become family." Cook came out then to join the three.

"Leaving?"

"Can't stay here. Too many look at me suspiciously when I'm here in the hills. Don't want those people to become distrustful of the caravan too. Still a lot of daylight. We'll head for the voyageurs camp just up the river. Should easily make that before nightfall."

"Laddie, I've lost two dish washers. Makes life rougher for me. Glad he's going with you. Hope the uncle can find you a patch of that *land of milk and honey*."

Little was said as Bjorn stepped up and gave Cook a bear hug and turned and did the same to Stone. Retrieving his bed roll always tied to the back of Cook's wagon, he placed it on Red behind his saddle.

"Just a minute," came from Cook as he went back into the hut. Returning with two leather sacs, he handed one to each. "Jerky and a biscuit or two for tonight's meal. Keep safe, laddies."

Goodbyes are never easy and Bjorn found this one especially hard, having grown to appreciate both men. Waving as they left, the two rode out of camp and headed for the upper trail on the other side of the tall grass that separated the dunes from the river's edge.

Chapter 25

Bjorn heard the singing before he and River reached their camp (north of Waverly today). The well-worn, tri-rutted trail leading to the camp and beyond meandered along the Mississippi River, giving evidence that oxen and horses had pulled many carts and wagons north and west.

Pig's Eye hadn't shared much about these French fur trappers and traders. What he did say was that they would know about Old Crossing. He couldn't wait to see if they knew Uncle Olaf. Riding in to camp, Bjorn counted five brightly dressed men sitting on logs around the campfire where a young deer roasted on a spit. The singing stopped as they came in view.

"River, *ça se fait*? (How come?) You're back," came from the one across the fire that saw them first. The rest turned and one by one greeted River with the traditional hand-forearm welcoming.

"Le blonde?" Pier asked.

"Bjorn Hanson. Looking to get to the Old Crossing. Has an uncle there."

"Bjorn. Uncle? Name?" asked another, the one closest to Bjorn.

"Olaf Seim." Know of him?"

"Seim. Hmmm. Seim. Heard of him?" he asked the rest. The others scratched their beards and looked blank. "Must not be a trapper. We know most of those."

"Going with him, River?" Pier questioned.

"Need to. Have medicine for Johnson, shop keeper there."

"Lucky for you, Bjorn. More here than we can eat," decided Pier, placing his trust in River that Bjorn was honest. "Tie those to a tree. Venison about ready. Smells good too."

Sitting on a log by the fire, Bjorn couldn't take his eyes off the colorful dress of these voyageurs. Each had a bright coarse blue cloth coat with a brighter sash tied around his waist. Beaded pouches hanging below the sash were visible, full of who knew what. Underneath the shirts were leather leggings and breeches. Moccasins covered their feet and laced up over the calf of the leg. Strength radiated from their bodies. Shoulders were broad and capable of stroking the paddles that moved the canoes great distances with each pull of the paddle. Their muscular legs were used to portage the canoe's. Each canoe could carry150 pounds over the roughest trail. No river or lake? They walked up to the armpit in the tall grass or brush with the loaded canoe hoisted on their shoulders. Three carts loaded with traded furs sat at the side of the campfire.

"Can you wait three days? We'll go back with you. More safety in numbers," said Pier, hoping to detain River.

"Could but don't want to. Promised to return as soon as I could. Want to keep my word."

"Any medicine you'd trade with us?" one of the quiet men asked?

"Already traded some away. Better keep what I have. If you see Delaware, ask him to go back to grandmother and get you some."

Stomachs filled, conversation lagged as tiredness of the day descended on group. Checking Red and Scout once more after taking care of his necessities, Bjorn took his bed roll and lay it near River, but did not undress. The coolness of the evening warranted cover and his clothes were just enough to make him feel comfortable.

"Where're you headed?" asked Pier.

"Hope to get to the Crow River Trading Post. Anything I should be aware of?" questioned River, knowing the group had just come through there.

"Quicker by boat. We'll buy the horses."

"Sorry. Need them up around the prairie grassland," said River. "Trail will have to do for a while."

"Thanks for the meal. When you come back to Old Crossing. Ask where I am. Come and see me. Maybe Uncle Olaf will have some wooden shoes to trade," suggested Bjorn.

"Shoes? You say wooden? We'll stop for sure. Wooden shoes last longer than these leather moccasins," decided Pier.

With bed rolls tied behind, the two started down the path once again. Here and there, pieces of ox carts littered the sides of the trail. "What happened here? Some kind of war?"

"No," came from River. "You'll see when we get there. The oxcarts on our train were better built than the Red River cart is."

"The difference?"

"Red River cart has a gearing shaft made of rawhide and wood. A single ox is harnessed to the shaft. The wheels are about six feet across, made entirely of wood from the largest tree found. The box is maybe three feet wide and seven feet long, balanced on those two wood wheels."

"What's the hub made of?"

"Wood too. Sometimes rawhide circles it, put on wet as a sealer of sorts."

"Does the hide seal the wheel to the hub? Doesn't the hide dry out?"

"Does. And then the wheels squeak unless they are kept greased."

Movement over the well-worn trail was an easy ride for the two of them, responsible only for themselves. Pieces of jerky Cook had supplied satisfied their hunger pangs. Water ran clear in the rivers and streams, sating thirst. The warm south breeze on their backs assured them that summer was around the corner. Bjorn hoped to either help Olaf plant or work somehow through the rest of this year to save money for a parcel of land. Uneasy feelings rumbled through his head, so unsure of this New World, knowing how green he was at clearing virgin land.

Chapter 26

Leaving the well-worn trail headed north and west along the Mississippi, the two veered left, taking what looked like a large deer trail that led into the woods. Bjorn wondered but didn't ask why they had left one trail and taken another, fully trusting River's judgment. Sometimes the horses jumped over logs covering the trail. At other times the two dismounted and physically moved the fallen trees or limbs off, clearing a path for travel. At one point, River said, "Trail leads to the Crow River, not often used as you see."

"Why the Crow?"

"We'll follow it 'til we get to the twin lakes west of here." He hadn't more than answered Bjorn when the thick overhanging trees were replaced with bushes laden with a small purple fruit and finally open prairie and gently rolling hills as far as the eye could see." Stopping Scout, River began stripping the fruit off the tree limbs and ate as fast as he could. "Good."

Bjorn did the same, surprised at the sweetness of the fruit and ate a little more cautiously when he saw how stained his hands were becoming. "Name?"

"We call them June berries. Bloom this time of year. These and the wild strawberries are the first fruits of the new year. Not far to Crow River now," and he led the way across the open prairie through green, lush grass as high as the haunches of the horses. Reaching a gentle rise in the land, the two stopped and viewed the Crow in front of them.

Bjorn pointed to a strange floating mass in the river and asked, "What's that? Looks like a cart floating."

"Is. The wheels of two carts are taken off. One or two buffalo hides are placed over the axels and tied on securely. It's a hide canoe that floats when it needs to and can be pulled by the voyageurs when the water is too shallow to float it."

"Can it hold much weight?"

"About a 1000 pounds if it needs to. The box is put on top of the robe and filled with the furs or whatever has been traded."

"Helps keep the wheels greased too, right."

"If the wood of the axel keeps swollen from water, the wheel's less likely to come off. You're right."

"See that clearing to the west of the canoe?"

"Ja."

"We'll spend the night there. As safe as any in this open prairie."

Once reaching the river, both men took care of their mounts and curried them, checked their hoofs, fed and watered them. River took his two bed roll blankets, found two three foot y sticks and a longer one, and anchored the shorter two standing upright in the ground. Next, he put the longer one over the two y's. The two blankets were thrown over the longer pole so that each hung in front and back of what would be the openings on each end of the simple tent.

Bjorn watched the process for a bit and then went, got his own sticks, and mimicked what he saw River do. "Why the flaps at the front and back?"

"Still cold at night. Helps keep the chill out. Use it for mosquitoes too but it's too early for them."

"Mosquitoes?"

"Just wait. You'll soon know. Let's fish for supper." He went to his pack and found a long thin rawhide and bent hook that had a feather attached at its top. Seeing an eddy, he aimed for its center and was not surprised when a large bass grabbed on and then flew out of the water, trying to shake the hook. In one quick motion, River leaned forward and then raised his arms high, causing the fish to fly up over his head and land on the bank behind him. Three more times he repeated this pattern and three more times fish flew up, over his head and behind on the bank.

Bjorn watched the first come out of the water and went to the bushes beside the river, selected sturdy limbs from the branches, and stripped them as best he could of leaves and bark. Coming back he said, "You fish. I cook this time." Each fish was gutted, beheaded and speared onto one of the stripped branches, ready to lay across the y branches at each side of the fire to cook. Remembering the biscuits Cook had given them, Bjorn went to his sack on the pommel, opened it and brought out the linen parcel. "Not too squashed. Be good with the fish," decided Bjorn as he walked back to the fire to tend his dinner.

With no moon, darkness came early and the two, filled with fish and biscuits, willingly crawled into their tents, glad of the warmth their tents provided from the north wind off the river.

Chapter 27

River had water boiling in a small container over an even smaller fire. His tent was dismantled, ready to load behind his saddle. Bjorn woke with a start, sensing dawn was near. "Need your cup." Bjorn reached in his pack, found his cup and handed it to him. "Like oatmeal?"

"*Ja*. Like the mush of home."

"Be a minute and we'll eat. Pack your tent so we can leave when we're done."

Bjorn did as asked and noticed some of yesterday's same berries on a bush nearby, picked what he could carry in his hands and returned to River and the small fire. Both cups had oatmeal in them. Bjorn took the berries and split them between the two cups, sat down and the two slowly enjoyed both. Finished, he took the two cups down to the river, scrubbed them clean with sand, rinsed them well and came back as River doused the fire with water from his jug, took a stick and covered the area well with the sand around the edges of the pit. "Won't fool everyone. Won't be as visible from the rise up there. Mount up and we'll see what today brings."

The trail today wasn't much different from the ones the caravan had taken. Difference was that there were less rough hills to climb, more sandy land, and more prairie. Patches of hard woods opened to expanses of open prairie where deer and an occasional bison roamed.

"What is that with the heavy fur across its shoulders" asked Bjorn who had never seen a bison.

"Tatanka ohitika. Brave Buffalo. Hope we get to hunt them before we get to Crossing."

"Are they like cattle?"

"But can be really mean and run much faster. Stampede easily. Thrill to hunt with a spear."

"Spear? No gun?"

"Always kill the old way. Much more honorable to the great spirit."

Each mile down the trail seem no different from the last. Woods, prairie, rolling hills, and now and again cool, clear water expansions to the sides of the trail and not far away. As the sun began to set, the river widened, becoming more lake than river. At its edge where it began to widen stood a hut. When the two came closer, Bjorn read, "Northwest Company Trading."

"We stop here tonight (Kingston MN today). Need to trade medicine for otter furs. Hudson Bay Company at Old Crossing pays well for them."

The two dismounted in front of the inn and handed the reins to a young lad about ten. "Curry, feed and water, for coins."

"Do that. We'll see how many coins when morning comes," said River to the lad as he rubbed his head.

"River," came from the opening. A short, toothless woman came towards him, ducking through doorway. She was half the doorway's height and about as wide. "Heading north again? Got medicine?"

"Many Furs. Always have medicine for you. This is Bjorn. Going to settle in the Northwest Territory."

"Welcome. Good thing I made lots of acorn mush. One Scar shot two geese. Make good mush. Come" and she turned, ducked under the door and entered, expecting they would do so also and they did.

"River," spoke a weathered face, seated at one side of the open cooking pit in the center of the hut that served as stove and heat. "Join the circle. You too. His friend is our friend."

"This is Bjorn. Going North. Has an Uncle somewhere around Old Crossing."

"Bjorn. Not common name."

"I came over on a schooner from the Old Country," he answered. "River is guiding me."

"You and many others come. Take our land away. Disturb our hunting."

"Enough." Many Furs ignored his grunting and continued. "Can't change what is. Only government can. Come. Sit. Eat. Mush gets cold" and she passed out bowls much like Pig's Eye had back on the trail, filled with a fragrant smelling mush. "Acorn mush. Squirrels and I fight each fall to see who can store the most." Bjorn hadn't eaten acorn mush before that he knew of. Didn't look much different in the bowl than the oatmeal Cook used or the mush he'd had on the schooner or at home. The boneless goose chunks were tender and the contents had an onion flavoring. Many Furs poured a peppermint tea into cups to drink and left the pot on the side of the fire pit to sip as needed.

Finishing the meal, River went to his bed roll, retrieved his satchel and extracted two medicine bags.

"No more?"

"Need the rest for Old Crossing. Promised more to them than I brought last time. Much sickness up there. New people don't know the old ways. No doctor. Need *Okomisan*'s medicine."

"Grandmother make good medicine," One Scar stated emphatically. "Bring us more next time."

"I'll do that . . ." and was interrupted by the young boy who came in the door, done caring for the two horses.

"In the morning, can I ride yours, River?"

"We'll see how well you cared for him."

"Rolls are on the log benches in the lean-to. Horses are in the next stall."

Rising, River thanked Many Furs and so did Bjorn, both commenting on the good meal. "We'll leave at daylight. No need to fix a meal for us."

"I'll have biscuits ready and some jerky too. Can't send grown men like you out without food."

"Appreciate that and I'll have more medicine for you next time." Ducking as they went out and closing the make-shift door, the two headed for the lean-to, their bed rolls and a night's sleep.

Chapter 28

Repacked and saddled up again, the two followed the river and the three-rutted trail for a distance until another veered off to the left and west. Ruts weren't as deep here so Bjorn decided that this trail was not the most traveled and wondered why.

"Heading west from here. See that mountain ridge (Powder Ridge MN today) over there?" he asked as he pointed out an overgrown hill to Bjorn.

"*Ja*. Small mountain to me."

"Got any room in your bed roll?"

"Some. Didn't pack much as you know."

"Room enough for two pair of shoes?"

"Shoes? There a trading post up the road?"

"No. Basswood trees."

"I've carved shoes with my uncle. Why basswood?"

"Light. Floats on water. Should make light shoes." Reaching the mountain edge, River chose a powdery path that led up in a winding fashion. The two horses took their time to pick their way up over the brambles and dislodged rock nature left on the trail.

"Glad we don't have a cart. Be a tough climb for oxen."

"Few come this way. Trail shows that. Old Ojibwa trail used by my people to get to other family at Osakis Lake. Trading post down there. See it?"

"Stopping?"

"Not here. Only long enough to cut four sections of a good basswood tree in that grove for the two pair of shoes I promised you."

"Trail gets rougher and want to get to Ceder Lake (Cold Spring MN area) by tomorrow night."

"Rock formations north of us look like small mountains to me. Need to cross them?"

"Not cross them so much as wind around them. Formations are a hard stone (granite). Deep pools form in some of the depressions. Good fishing."

The two talked little once they reached the rocks and boulders. Red, startled by a deer that darted away from a small pooled depression on the left of the trail, reared unexpectedly and threw Bjorn off. Bjorn landed on his back on the same left side the deer ran from and hit his head on a sharp rock. Reaching up to hold his head as he tried to rise, his hand became wet.

Hearing Red's neighing warning, River turned back in the saddle and witnessed the fall. Quickly halting Scout, he dismounted and raced back the short distance to Bjorn, lying face up against the rocks on the trail behind. Blood greeted him. "Head wound. The worst kind out here," he thought. Racing back to his pommel, he took the medicine bag, his water jar along with a small blanket he always carried and returned as fast to Bjorn. Laying the blanket near where Bjorn lay, River turned him over so he could see the wounded area now bleeding profusely. Opening the bag, he extracted padding, a bag of medicine, and a knife incased in a leather covering. Cutting hair away from the wound, he took one of the pads, added drops of a liquid from one of the bottles, and held the pad to the slash the rock made in the scalp. Repeating the process twice – new pad with medicine and pressure – finally lessened the bleeding to a slight flow. Bjorn continued to breathe normally but did not move. Cleaning the area of hair and cutting more away from the open gash, River took a clean medicine pad, placed it on the wound. Using longer strips he removed from the bag, he wrapped Bjorn's head so the pad would stay in place. Satisfied he'd done as much as he could, he left him to lie there, knowing he'd need to find a cave area close.

Leaving Scout, he scaled the rock formations near them and spotted an overhang farther down the trail. Returning to Bjorn who still lay in the same position, he called Scout to his side and removed the saddle. Taking Bjorn's arms, River hefted him on to his shoulders and just as carefully placed him across Scout on the blanket where the saddle had been. Bjorn remained limp, unaware. Leading Scout down the trail, River realized Red followed behind, unaffected by the scare.

Reaching the overhung area, he softly sang as he looked into the caved area just beyond the ledge above. "*Nagi tanka* (Great Spirit), you watch over us!" Leaving Bjorn atop Scout, River raced to the opening, saw no animals in it, and returned to Bjorn. Coaxing Scout to come as close to the cave as possible, he maneuvered the horse so that when he carried Bjorn to the cave entrance, the distance would be as short as possible. Taking him off Scout's shoulders wasn't as easy as placing him there. Allowing Bjorn's limp body to slip down along with the saddle blanket, River grabbed the arms when he could, protecting the head as much as possible and slung him over his right shoulder as best he could, letting the feet drag. He knelt at the entrance on a rain-cleaned slab of rock and laid Bjorn down. Scout stood where he'd left him and so did Red, both sensing something was wrong.

Realizing Bjorn probably wouldn't move very far if at all, River tended to the horses. A patch of grass grew to the side of the cave, situated on a very small plateau at the base of more rock boulders. Clean water, gathered in a pool would quench their thirst. He hobbled both, not quite sure what animals might be around and cause them to jolt. Next, he retrieved his saddle from where Bjorn had fallen and carried it back up the hill to the cave. Bjorn lay still in the same position. "Need to get our packs and blankets into the cave. Might be a while," he said as he sorted out in his mind what the next few hours might mean for them.

Breaking off a leafed branch from a nearby bush, River entered the cave, went to the back of it and swept the floor clean, or as clean as possible using this makeshift broom. "Someone's used this overhang before. Spot here is where they had a fire going," he decided in his mind. Surprised at the depth of the cave area, he raised his hands to the sky and once again said, "*Nagi tanka* (Great Spirit), you watch over us! Time to prepare for a stay."

Back to the horses he went and removed all but the halter and lead ropes of each horse. Blankets, bed rolls, pouches, water jars, and whatever else each animal carried he carried into the cave trip by trip back up. The overhang and cave would be home until Bjorn recovered enough to ride. The stash made quite a pile in the middle of the cave entrance. Taking the two saddle blankets and two of the four blankets they had with, he fashioned a bed on an even area away from the glare of the sun and out of the swirling wind. Finished, he returned to Bjorn, stood behind his head and reached under his shoulders, pulling him over to the bed that would be his. A groan came from the man just as River began to pull. Once more "*Nagi tanka* (Great Spirit), you watch over us" came from River, glad to hear some response from the white man he'd grown to love and trust as a brother. Carefully he laid Bjorn on his side on the blankets, not wanting to disturb the wound. Resting a bit and drinking from Bjorn's water jar, he looked out and saw the sun wending its way to the base of the horizon and knew that there was little daylight left.

Leaving Bjorn and the rest of the pile still in the middle of the cave opening, River searched for kindling and wood, scanned the area as he did, looking for others that may be in the area – wagon trains, trappers, traders, or natives. He saw no movement below or above the little he could see up and around all the boulders overhead and returned to the cave with the firewood. Squirrels darted here and there, searching for spring replenishment of their exhausted winter acorn supply. Grabbing Bjorn's slingshot and two pebbles, two scurrying by became supper.

Arranging the rest of their belongings didn't take long. They had little with them. Bjorn stirred again and River went to him, checked the wound for bleeding and was satisfied that the wound's bandaged area was relatively dry. "Fire is next," he mumbled softly to himself.

An hour passed quickly and so did the sun's dropping over the horizon. Moonlight filtered through the brush on each side of the cave and created eerie shadows. The small fire illuminated the cave's interior enough so that River knew animals would be wary. Skinning the squirrels, gutting them and placing each on a hot rock at the edge of the small fire took little time. River had been well schooled by the elders. Using some of the water from the jar he always carried on the pommel, he made an herb broth he hoped to get Bjorn to drink when he woke.

Chapter 29

The smell of food does wonders! As the squirrels baked on the hot rocks, their aroma filled the cave. Bjorn stirred and shifted so he lay on his back. Doing so caused pain and jolted him awake enough so he moaned and reached for the wounded area with his right hand. River grabbed the hand and said, "Bjorn. Easy. Lay still. You've hit your head and have quite a slash on the back. Need to rest."

Sensing River by his side and somehow understanding what was said, Bjorn relaxed again but lay on his opposite side, using an arm for a pillow. River let him rest that way for a while and then decided to see if he could get some of the herb broth made from crushed birch bark in him. Placing the cup within reach, River nudged Bjorn. "Bjorn. Bjorn. Do you hear me? Need to drink this tea. Will help the healing. I'll protect your head."

Slowly but with determination registering on his face, Bjorn turned on his back, trusting River to protect he wounded area, and found himself cradled in his arms. "Tukk," rumbled quietly from him as he settled back against River's chest.

"Drink. Need strength. Lost quite a bit of blood. Help you heal." Small sips disappeared each time the drink reached Bjorn's lips. The effort it took for Bjorn to do so tired him again and he fell back asleep. River laid him back on his side on the bed and covered him with one of the blankets.

River slept little through the night, awaking whenever Bjorn shifted positions in his sleep. Bjorn drank the tea each time River woke him and each time fell asleep in River's arms. As the sunlight replaced the moonlight filtering through the same bushes in front of the cave, River jerked awake, hearing his name.

"Riv. Riv. Here?"

Scrambling around the fire and over to him, he saw Bjorn attempting to sit. "Careful. Don't stand. Sit."

Sitting with his legs crossed in front of him, he said, "How bad?"

"Enough so I had to scalp you," offered River with a smile on his face.

"Scalp?" and he reached to touch the bandage on the back that covered the wound now throbbing.

"Rock you hit when Red reared and threw you put quite a gash in the back of your head. Had to cut some of the hair around away. You'll have a scar about four inches when it heals."

"Reared? Never done that."

"Doe scared her. Came across the path in front so close she couldn't avoid it unless she reared."

"Hurt?" concerned about his horse.

"No. Not like you. Let me see what it looks like today," and Bjorn leaned his head forward as River unwound the bandaging. Finding the pad stuck to the wound, he said, "Need to heat the herb water so I can soak the bandage off. Don't want the bleeding to start again. Hungry?"

"No. More thirsty."

"Drink the tea. If you get sleepy, put your head on your arms in your lap so I can see to the wound." Instructions given, River went to the medicine bag, found more crushed birch bark, put some in the cup with water and set it by the fire to heat. Digging in the medicine bag, he found a small piece of intestine tied at both ends. He knew this was the *Okomisan's* bayberry mixed with fat that she used on open wounds to make them heal faster.

Taking a clean pad, he took his knife, opened the intestine, and smeared the contents that spilled out onto the linen pad.

"Tired."

"Need to soak this old pad off and replace it with new. Might hurt when I pull it off if I can't get it soaked free."

"Throbs now."

"Tea should take care of that. Need to sleep. Sleep makes body heal faster according to grandmother." River continued to talk, saying nothing meaningful but trying to keep Bjorn's mind off of what he was doing. Freeing the bandage took time but it came off cleanly and the wound beginning to scab looked good. Snipping a strand or two of hair went unnoticed by Bjorn, as asleep as he could be sitting with his head in his hands like River had instructed. Retying the bandage by winding the strips around the head was the only way to keep the pad in place. Satisfied he'd done what he could, Bjorn groaned in pain when River helped him lay down again.

Evening shadows returned to replace the sun's rays. Fire smoldered under a rabbit River snared close to the horses he continued to check on. Knowing they needed to exercise, he unhobbled first one and then the other, rode them bareback for a distance down and up again to their private patch of grass and watering hole.

Returning back to the cave, he was surprised to see Bjorn sitting. "Need to go outside."

"Let me help. Need to stand a bit if you can before you try walk." Going behind, he lifted under the armpits and Bjorn stood. "Steady. Hurt?"

"Throbs. Not as bad as it has. Dizziness gone. Let's see if I can make it outside." Slow steps took him to the cave entrance and a little farther out where he took care of his necessities. Sweat poured off him as he struggled to stay conscious and on his feet. "Back before I fall."

"Need to eat before you sleep again," stated River in a firm voice. "Rabbit. More tea here in the cup."

Bjorn ate a little, dosed a little, was awaked by River and told to eat. With half of the haunch of the rabbit and the tea drunk, River relented and let him lie back and sleep. Two days passed and the patterned continued. The only change in each day was the meat offered, depending on what River snared or shot.

Chapter 30

Early in the morning of the fourth day, River was seeing to the horses and was startled when Red neighed. Looking down, he saw no movement. Scout did not seem at all disturbed. Looking up to the cave, he was surprised to see Bjorn sitting on a rock just outside the opening. "Better?" he asked when he got back to the entrance.

"Much. Think I'll live. Wasn't sure for a while. How does it look?"

"Last I looked, it had scabbed over good. Didn't want to take the bandage off. Scared you scratch it open or bump it open in your tossing about. Let's take a look."

"Been a nuisance?"

"No more than your usual green," chuckled River, continuing to free the wrappings.

"How many days have we lost?"

"Today is the fourth."

"If I'm healed, can we pack and leave?"

"Looks good," was his comment when the wound was visible. "Better spend the day and night here. You need to sit, walk – be on your feet before you try and ride over this rocky area. It's a ways before we get to the *Osaki-zibi* (Sauk River to the Chippewa)."

"*Osaki-zibi*?"

"The Sauk River where three trails split off. One along the Mississippi, one west, and one north and west."

"Which one do we take?"

"The one west. Want to leave the wound to open air so it will scab better. Don't scratch. Keep your hair out of it. Hungry?"

"Jerky?"

"Your slingshot works good," and he smiled as he took it out of his back pocket. "Hit a coon. Just got it skinned when Red neighed. Wondered what bothered him and then I saw you up here." Going to one of the bushes that had sturdier branches coming from the roots, River cut three, came back to Bjorn and handed them over to him. "Take the bark off while I go get the critter" and he left Bjorn struggling to peal the branch of its outer covering.

The two spent the rest of the day watching birds swoop, an occasional deer roam from one place to another, and a fox come close enough to see who the newcomers were. Bjorn made himself walk and his first walk was to visit Red who nuzzled his pocket, looking for a treat. "Sorry, gal. Didn't come prepared. Will have something for you next time." Soft neighing sounds came from her as he rubbed the area between eyes and nose tip. Walking back up to the cave opening taxed his strength so much he went back to his bed roll, leaned against the wall and slept until the smell of roasting meat awakened him from his dreams.

"We'll pack as much as we can and leave in the morning if you feel up to it. What do you think?"

"Won't know until I'm in the saddle, I suppose. Can't stay here forever. Lucky you found this place for us."

"I didn't"

"What do you mean you didn't?"

"*Nagi Tanka* did."

"*Nagi Tanka*?

"Great Spirit found if for us. Healed you too."

Rumbling sounds came from the west. River climbed to see what the cause was and saw the dark clouds approaching. Scrambling down to the horses, he unhobbled both and brought them up to the cave entrance. Bjorn had cleared an area for them under the overhang.

Just as quickly as the storm came over the rocky hillside, it passed over but not until it left small hail stones in its wake. Neither horse felt the storm's impact standing under the overhang that protected them. "We'll leave them here. Make packing quicker," decided River. "How's the head?"

"Itches where the scab is. Must mean its healing. I'll put my stocking cap on to protect it. Least it doesn't throb anymore."

"Get some sleep. You'll need it. Don't know how weak you are. Didn't eat much. Too tired from the tea." Without argument, River watched Bjorn go to the bed roll and lay down, using one of the blankets as a pillow.

Chapter 31

The gentle loping of the horse's pace went smoothly for Bjorn until he began to tire. Each soft gallop down the trail became a jolt to the body, especially the head, and the pounding he'd experienced came back to haunt him. Once out of the boulders and rock, the trail followed high ridges to avoid the swamp, ponds and small lakes that spread across the land. In the distance River pointed out a cart trail. Riding over another ridge, Bjorn saw the Sauk meandering its way through small forest areas, open prairie and marsh. "Hut's Post is there where the three trails join. See it?"

"Looks bigger than most."

"Is. Because the three trails meet here. Some wait for a train to go their direction. Some set up shops to sell wares to those passing through. Others got tired of being on the trail and stopped here. Fishing's good. Deep in spots. Plentiful. So's trapping. Both companies come here to trade."

"Staying tonight?"

"Wasn't but think we should. You've done well. Head hurt?"

"Some. Expected it to. Keep the hair you cut off to trade?" asked Bjorn with a smile on his face.

"Didn't amount to much or I would have. Looks funny now. It'll grow back. Took off as little I could and yet clean the area.

Rounding a bend, both horses stopped. A cart River recognized as a voyageur's cart stood in the middle of the trail, wheel off.

"Francois? That you?"

"*Oui* (yes) and troubles too."

Both men dismounted and came close to the cart, wheel off and cracked in two. "Hit that rock just right, see it? Cracked the wheel. Not sure what to do."

"Got a long rope?" asked River.

"*Oui*. What for?" and he reached in his cart and handed it to River.

Taking the rope, he attached one end to the axel of the wheel still intact. He threw the rest of the rope under the cart hard enough so it was visible on the other side. Grabbing the rope when he came around, he kept it in his hand as he remounted. "Get her to turn around," ordered River of Francois. Her was the ox that stood patiently waiting. River put tension on the rope and pulled until Scout was alongside the cart, acting like the missing wheel. "We'll be your wheel until you get back to the Sauk."

Reaching the outskirts of the small village formed along the banks of the Sauk where the three trails met, Francois stopped and so did Scout. Releasing the rope, River shook hands with the Frenchman, wished him well, and continued with Bjorn along the West trail to the edge of the encampment where a small inn stood. Turning to Bjorn now beside him on Red he said, "See if there's a room. Should be welcome here too but you be the judge. It'll depend on who else is staying. Horses need a place too. I'll go water them and let them graze along the bank over there."

Two Ojibwa from the looks of their clothing sat at the fire eating whatever was in the pot. "Bed?" asked a small, grizzled man who'd just laid another log on the fire.

"Two of us. And horses."

"Those ropes are yours. Bring in your own blankets. Chicken stew in the pot if you're hungry. Biscuits in the morning. Pay me then too." No more was asked of Bjorn. No more was said and he turned his back on all three as he went back out the reed-woven door.

River was outside now. "Ropes to sleep on. Bring in blankets. Chicken stew in the pot for tonight and biscuits in the morning. Two Ojibwa I think they are sitting and eating in front of the fire. I'll go back in first. That way you can look the two over before they see you."

Entering, River stopped, looked at the two and said, "Rising Moon. Quail." The two rose, came towards River and clasped hands.

"On the road north?" asked Quail.

"With Bjorn. Wants to get to Old Crossing. Uncle there. Told the land is *milk and honey*."

"Quail. Rising Moon," spoke Bjorn as he clasped each hand.

"Just in time for the buffalo hunt. Need to wait for Stripped Feather. Coming down from the north trail. Scouting for a small oxcart train."

"Wait with us?" asked Rising Moon.

"Need to move on. Need to get *Okomisan's* medicine to Old Crossing. Promised Bjorn I'd help him find his Uncle there."

"Morning comes early. Sleep," came with another hand clasping from Rising Moon.

Ropes squeaked and complained when the four men placed their blankets on top and rolled on the suspended beds handing from the sturdy rafters of the thatched ceiling.

Chapter 32

Sitting easier in the saddle today with fewer sharp pains radiating from his head, Bjorn marveled at the changing scenery, so different from the Old Country. The meadows rolled north to the Mississippi River from the *Osaki-zibi.* The falls they'd seen reminded him of the mountain run off in his Nordic homeland and made him lonesome. At times the prairie opened its wide expanse, so wide it was more like a green ocean. Just as quickly it would enter a large oak grove as it did now on the trail in front of them.

Buzzing. Birds? Can't be. Too small. One landed on a knuckle on his hand, he felt a sting and he slapped at it, surprised at the blood streak it left. The midday winged insects rose in swarms around him seeking food, not caring where they lit. Then he remembered River's warning, "Mosquitos. You'll learn about them soon enough." Bjorn's slapping brought strawberry-colored bumps on his skin. The more he slapped the more came to light. Red felt the winged intrusions bite his ears. River was being bitten too he noticed and urged Scout into a faster trot. Both horses and men felt relief when sun streamed in front of them on the trail and the wind blew against their faces. Out and away a distance, River halted Scout, turned to Bjorn as he came aside and said, "Mosquitoes. Worst pest this country has. Woodticks are easier to deal with."

"Mosquitoes? Woodticks?"

"Mosquitoes hatch in open water, live a short time and love to suck blood from beast and man. Woodticks hatch in the spring but last a shorter season than the mosquitoes. Ticks don't make noise like the mosquitoes. They just crawl all over you and bite too. Remember when I had you use the two blankets to cover the entrance to the tent we each made?"

"*Ja.*"

"Thought we'd have mosquitoes that night. Didn't. Our smoky fire probably keep them away. Be glad the wind is blowing. Help's too."

One day seem to blend into the next. Mosquitoes. Swamp. Ridges to ride. Open prairie with grass as high as the haunches of the horses. A gopher hole the horse knew enough to avoid. The trail bent northwestward and followed a ridge until a lake was visible in the distance. River, riding ahead, spotted two on horseback, signaled Bjorn to halt and he did. Just as suddenly a piercing bird cry erupted from River, and Bjorn watched as the two riders turned, voiced the same shrill cry and waited. River motioned him to follow. Riding closer, Bjorn watched the two ahead raise a gun in a hand and hold it high in the air.

"River. Medicine. Good," rattled out of a deep, rumbling voice of the one called Shale.

"Guns? Trouble?"

"Him?" asked the other who Bjorn found out later was named Blue Sky.

"Bjorn. Guiding him to Old Crossing. Uncle there. Good man. Like a brother to Delaware and me. Came from the Old Country. Not like some who come."

"*Nadous-sioux* come north. Trappers traded with us for guns. Protect us," offered Blue Sky.

"Kill too," warned River. "Hide them. Use only when you need to for protection."

"Use at buffalo hunt," decided Shale.

"No. Not like the old ways. Upset too many of our people," warned Blue Sky, hoping to change the younger brave's mind. "Where're you headed?"

"Not sure how far."

"Camp with us tonight before you go up the trail to Lobster Lake," suggested Blue Sky and he turned his horse towards the lake and the crude huts along its shore.

Fish smoking on the wet planks next to the fire greeted them as they entered the small clearing by the lake. Four huts, one for each, stood near the fire pit. Caring for the horses came first, each tending the one ridden. Bjorn still itched from the mosquito bites so he went to the shore of the lake, stripped off his clothes and dove in to the cool clear water. Swimming a while eased the tension of the day and cleaned not only his body but his soul. "River. What would I do without him?" he thought as he swam back and dressed. He joined the three sitting beside the fire.

Rain came in torrents on the thatched roofs of the huts in the early dawn of morning. As crude as those huts looked from the hill, Bjorn and his bed roll were not wet. Built on a slight mound, the rain flowed around and away, down to the lakeshore. He saw the others sitting in the openings, watching, waiting, wondering when the shower would end. He spent the time repairing a hole in his shoe near his instep. Wondering how it got there, he decided it probably came from his falling off Red when she reared. Finding his needle in his pack, he took the cording he'd brought along, threaded it into the needle and sewed the opening slash together as cleanly as he could. "BOOM!" came out of nowhere. "A gunshot?" Bjorn moved back into the shadow of his hut and watched the doors of the two other huts, visible to him from where he sat.

Blue Sky was first to move towards the sound and was obviously angry when he saw Shale come from the lake carrying a goose. Too far away to hear their conversation and unable to understand them as they talked their Ojibwa language, he quickly repacked and wrapped his bed roll so he'd be ready to leave in short notice. Looking across, he saw River heft both his pack and bed roll up in his arms, stand and head toward the horses. Bjorn did the same, reached Red, secured his belongings once he saddled her, and mounted. The two left and headed down the west trail towards another lake River called Lobster.

Chapter 33

Gentle rain showers persisted now and again but the mosquitoes left them alone. A warm breeze quickly dried the droplets. A dog barked and a wolf howled, sounds Bjorn was familiar with from the Nordic Mountains. River stopped ahead as they reached a narrow but very boggy spot. The horses were allowed to go at their own speed and soon were across to the other side and hard ground, unaffected by the recent rains.

Bjorn looked in front of him and marveled at the expanse of rolling prairie. Openings in the grass that reached to the horse's haunches on the side of the trail led to small wooded areas where he was sure animals looked out at them, disturbing their peace. The soft loping of the horses broke the silence and an occasional *Kill-dee, Kill-dee* of the killdeer flitting here and there around them warned of their intrusion.

Reaching a ridge, the two rode its crest as much as possible, avoiding the swamp and pesky mosquitoes. From this ridge Bjorn spotted what he knew must be Lobster Lake, so named he was sure because it did look like the lobsters he'd seen as he left the schooner. The claws reached north with the body portion mostly open water at the south end, the end they were headed towards.

Coming closer, River heard a wailing sound. Dismounting and handing Scout's reins to Bjorn, he crawled to where he thought the sound came from. More wailing. Peeking between the leaves of a bush he saw a trapper, leaning up against a tree, holding his stomach. Rising and signaling for Bjorn to come, he walked into camp.

"Ill?" questioned River as he stood in front of the young trapper.

"Very. Bad meat, I'd guess. Pains." Words came with effort as sweat poured from his face.

"How long you been sick?" questioned River as Bjorn came close and joined him.

"Three days. Keep nothing down. Not even water."

Bjorn busied himself getting a fire going and fetching water from the clear lake. River dug in his bag, retrieved another of *Okomisan's* medicine bags, dwindling fast with all the curing he'd done along the trail. Finding the angelica leaves in a pouch, he took enough to make a strong brew, placed them in a cup of water Bjorn had set near the fire to boil and waited. Removing it from the fire to cool, he delayed a bit and then went to the young man's side. "I'm River. He's Bjorn. Came from Carter's Cove and are going to Old Crossing. You?"

"Simon Pettre. Trapper for the Hudson Bay Company," came in fits and gasps from the young man clutching his stomach.

"Little far south for them, aren't you?"

"Got lost."

"Where you headed?" asked River.

Need to find the Mississippi. Need to head north.

"Sip this. I made Angelica tea. My okomisan, Grandmother, is medicine woman for my tribe." River sat back and watched as Simon sipped, and stopped moaning so much, glad help found him.

River stayed by the young trapper's side. Bjorn went to his pack, retrieved his fishing hook and line, and wandered to the lake, hoping to catch enough fish for the three of them. Colorful flat fish with body larger than an outstretched palm connected to a short fan tail bit the berries he used for bait. He quit when thirteen lay on the bank behind him – four for each to eat and one for him to learn to skin and debone. The trick was to slide the knife along the ribs of the fish, leaving white flesh. This much he knew from cleaning fish in the Old Country. He grabbed the smallest of the fish to practice on to discover where the rib bones were and how much flesh each fish had. It was a slow process for him because he had to be so careful where he cut to remove the bones and still keep the flesh in one piece. Taking his cleaned catch now lying on a handy piece of birch bark, Bjorn walked back to the fire he'd started.

"Pan. Lard there," offered Simon. "Biscuits in one of the tins."

"Must be feeling better or you wouldn't be interested in food," was Bjorn's comment as he reached for the pan.

"Still pain. Getting better. Don't feel like I'm going to heave my insides out like I did."

"I have peppermint syrup if you still have troubles," said Bjorn.

"I'll trade for it," came from the trapper, always ready to deal.

"Let's see how eating fish goes," decided River, grabbing tinware from the trapper's opened parcel and handing each their share of fried fish and a few biscuits from the tin.

"If you're going west on this trail, you'll need to ride farther around the lake or cross the corduroy road built over one of the bogs."

"Corduroy road. How do you make such a road?" asked Bjorn, always eager to learn new ways in this New World.

"Cut logs and lay them down as close as you can over the bog. Works good to pull carts and wagons over. Horses and oxen have trouble. Legs can get tangled in between the logs. Think we'll try it. Let the horses take their own pace. They know better than we what's under the water. Let's get some sleep. Morning comes early. Each day is a new challenge."

Simon woke, feeling so much better and gave River one of his best pelts for his doctoring. "Neither of you'll trade for you medicine?"

"I can't. Don't know what's ahead," stated Bjorn.

"Promised it to others farther north if I still have some left when we get there. Used a few packets along the trail. Thanks for the bog warning. We'll be watching for it." With a wave, River guided Scout back on the trail and Bjorn followed on Red.

A rich-looking land spread out in front of them as they cleared the small grove of trees that surrounded the lake. Clouds boiled overhead, more beautiful than threatening. A harsh land at times. Miles of it. A stretch of waving green interrupted by small ponds, few trees on rolling prairie. Reaching the bog, both horses slowed their pace, plunged in belly deep and continued forward, feeling their way with each slow step. Red's back left leg slipped once and Bjorn lowered his body to grab her mane for balance. Her next step or two found solid footing but Bjorn continued to lie forward to help balance the weight. Reaching solid ground, both horses resumed their gentle trot without encouragement and soon the two were on a hogback again.

Two rivers were visible in front of them. The Chippewa flowed south of them but far in the distance. The Pomme de Terre flowed from its namesake lake. From the names, Bjorn became aware of how much the tribes, trappers and voyageurs must roam this territory.

Frenchmen named the Pomme de Terre Lake and its namesake river using a French word meaning *apple of the earth*. The Pomme was a root vegetable, probably a turnip that grew wild and had eyes like a potato. Simon had a bag of them when Bjorn looked for food before he went fishing. He could see the river wind, bend, and flow south. "Where's the river go?"

"It meanders into and out of many clear lakes and marshes. Good place to hunt the birds that nest up and down its banks."

Fifteen minutes later they loped gently along the curving trail. A hill loomed in front of them, one the horses easily climbed, and another stream lay ahead. "A fork of the Chippewa," announced River as the horses splashed through the shallow water and leaped up the bank on the other side.

"Campsite," said Bjorn as he pointed downstream to several pole frameworks placed in a circle with their tops coming together at the center tip.

"Sioux." River pointed out. "Gone. Last year's tents. Couple of braves came to hunt *tipsinah* (wild potatoes) and their women built the tents. Might have hunted ducks or geese."

"Big structures," decided Bjorn.

"Takes four good sized skins," he commented as they continued down the trail. "Sand bar up ahead." Here the Chippewa widened with a small island in the middle. The horses found solid footing on the yellowish island. River stopped before entering the water on the other side of the bar and studied the flow. "Few rocks. Don't see a sinkhole. Bottom looks solid" and he urged Scout into the water. Clouds hung low and dusk came quickly on them so they stopped in a secluded copse next to the river, grateful for the soft breeze that kept most of the mosquitoes at bay.

Chapter 34

Bjorn watched and saw Scout's heels dig into the earth, climbing a rare steep rise in the land. The soil he kicked up was not the rocky sand of the trail they'd come but black and earthy. Heavy. He stopped a minute, reached way down and picked up a lump to crumble. The moist, rich soil left black marks on his hands. "Hope the soil at Old Crossing is this good," mumbled Bjorn.

They avoided the swamp to the east and continued riding the ridge until they saw a grey, choppy body of water shaped like a man's elbow (Elbow Lake). Ducks and geese feeding in the bay scattered when the two came close. Swans followed, stretching their necks as they rose above the water. The country rolled away. River guided them through gullies, ravines, and hogbacks, all the while heading west.

"When we reach the Shaved Prairies, we'll camp for the night and rest the horses. The buffalo hunt is in two days, I think," said River over the noise of the galloping horses. "Not sure if the Sioux are around. Don't want to find out either so we'll keep a little faster pace."

"Wonder what he means by shaved prairies?" thought Bjorn but he had little time to ponder. Narrow ridges, tracks made by carts and wagons, washouts from rain, and deadfalls kept both riders alert. On top of one of the ridges, River stopped. A long narrow strip that ran down a level area to water lay in front of them.

"Bay's called Lightning. See that trail. Leads to a stony fording. One of the few places we can cross this lake where there's a solid bottom. A lot of the lake is muck." To the right was a hill. To the left flowering vetch extended to the lake where whitecaps slapped at the shore. Nearing the ford, a cottonwood, hit by lightning, reached its splinters upward.

The ford provided a place to cross through brush and the wild overgrown grasses. Clouds darkened overhead and thunder rolled. The two headed for the canopied foliage of the maple and oaks in the distance. Here they waited under a leafy shelter, thick enough so drops did not reach them.

Drumming? Bjorn was off his horse in a flash and freed his slingshot from its pouch all in the same motion. Grabbed two stones. Set them and shot twice.

"Good. Food and no noise," said River as he watched two partridges, now kicking fluffs of feathers, flop limply. "Trees'll hid our fire. Smoke won't travel far with the heavy air. You got them. I'll cook them."

Night found them lying on beds of leaves and small branches, sated from the slow roasting of the two birds. Now and again the hoot of an owl or the howl of a coyote broke the silence and added to the swishing of the soft wind that disturbed the tree's branches. A raccoon came visiting in the early morning hours, headed to the lake to find clams and crayfish for breakfast.

Dawn broke cloudy but placid and the two struggled to use a trail that River recognized by the scat as a deer trail through the woods. Only once did they have to stop and clear a larger path. When they saw sunrays at the edge, they moved towards it only to find that the scrub brush had nettles. Bjorn's hatchet and expertise gained in cutting wood for Cook came in handy and he quickly cleaned a path. Once out in the open, he gaped at the wide expanse, level and smooth, bigger than any he'd seen so far. An ocean faced him, not the bluish gray of water but the greenish-gray of grass and creeping plants he had no names for. Shaved prairies. Land. Unoccupied. New. Untouched. Empty. All one needed to do was cross the river that ran red in front of them.

Chapter 35

"It's started," came from River in an almost reverent voice. "See the herd? See the grass move? See the buffalo pound in the distance?"

Bjorn stared hard, saw the herd peacefully grazing but did not at first see the movement in the grass. Watching the grey-green expanse in front of them for change, he concentrated hard and could see subtle movement and an arc forming. Well trained horses kept their heads down with their riders lying low over their backs. They continued to move the arc in the direction downwind of the herd that did not sense the intruders. The *pound*, Bjorn saw barely visible in the distance, looked like a chute that led to a corral made of rocks and branches – a trap for the bison.

"Too late to join them," decided River.

Bjorn was content to sit here on the hogback and watch as the hunt unfolded in front of them. Fifteen riders were now visible behind the small herd but still had not affected their grazing, so quiet was the approach. Cool, collected and watchful, each rider formed the curve so that once the stampede began, the bison would head in front of them into the chute that would trap them in the corral. With a signal from the center, the arc moved swiftly in mass charging the buffalo. Few turned on the riders and those that did were dodged and let through the arc. Bjorn felt the pulsing thunder in the ground caused by the herd's mass stampede. Once the braves had most of the herd gathered in the corral, they carefully culled it by selecting the five they wanted to kill, drew their bows and arrows and did so. Gored in the leg by one of the horns, one rider flew off his horse and just as quickly was picked up by another, taken out of the mayhem, and dropped beside a bison lying dead. River motioned to Bjorn to follow which he did. When they reached the place where the wounded brave lay, the two dismounted to help.

The size of the bison surprised Bjorn as he dismounted beside the animal and held the reins of both skittish horses, unaccustomed to the chaos of the few bison still lumbering around them.

"Otter, that you? Hurt bad?"

"River? Grazed, I think. No puncture."

Taking his knife, River sliced through what was left of the legging and exposed a gash about a hand's length on the outer side of the leg. Bjorn handed him his medicine pouch that hung from Scout's saddle. Removing a small casing containing a bayberry decoction, he used the liquid to wet a padding from the pouch and gently cleaned the reddened area. A small puncture was visible where the horn had first met flesh. The rest of the area seemed skinned, not ripped open. Extracting another casing, River let some of the contents flow on the wounded area. Satisfied that he'd done what was necessary, he pulled the bag's cording shut and handed it back to Bjorn.

"Always around when I need you," came from Otter with a smile on his face.

"A ways away from the Mississippi. More of your group here?"

"Five of us. Enough to take this one back to the band," pointing to the critter lying beside him. "Feed us for a while." Looking at Bjorn, he said, "I'll tell the rest to leave those curls alone. Need help, one of us will lend a hand." Rising, Otter whistled and his horse came from the edge of the corral.

With the kill completed, the effort had just begun. Working in units, the braves first skinned the buffalo in order to get at the meat. The portion down the center just below the surface of the back, known as the *hatched area,* had the more tender meat. It was treated reverently, and placed on a section of skin to be cared for later. Next the braves cut off the front legs and the shoulder blades, exposing the hump meat. They continued the butchering and removed the ribs. They saved some of the inner organs to use as containers once rinsed clean. Cutting the pelvis and hind legs off meant the neck and head, as one, still lay intact. Whatever smaller bit of meat that was picked away from the carcass lay on a small skin to become *pemmican.*

Two braves went back to the campsite and retrieved the travois so that the meat could be loaded and returned to camp for processing.

Quail came towards them. "Come to camp and share the heart and liver with us."

Bjorn looked at River and he spoke, "Thank you for your offer. Lot of daylight still ahead. Think we'll follow the Red north." The two remounted, signaled goodbye and rode to the river and the trail, headed for Old Crossing. Pausing briefly, they stopped at the river's edge and washed off the blood from the meat processing.

"Land is so different here. The soil is solid, heavy and black but the river sand is red and the water runs north from here, not like the Mississippi that ran south."

"You'll find that anything traded for and going up river is sold to the Hudson Bay trappers and traders. Northwest Company gets its stash from the rivers that flow south to the Mississippi."

"Heard one of the braves talk about an otter's tail," commented Bjorn.

"Otter Tail is the name of a river to the west of here and part of a lake. The Red River feeds from the Otter Tail River to the west and north. The Bois de Sioux River you saw from the ridge comes from the east and south of here. We will follow the Red north until we get to Old Crossing."

"A long ride from here?" came from Bjorn who realized his dream of seeing Uncle Olaf and the promised *milk and honey* land was close now.

"Should reach Crossing by nightfall." The two mounted and the horses loped easily along the oxcart trail that continued north along the river.

Few trees grew on the west side of the river where a high grey-green sea stretched to the horizon. The peaceful chirping of an occasional bird broke the quietness as the two loped along. River signaled to stop and they led the horses down to the river edge to water. Reaching in their pouches for the stale biscuits and *pemmican*, the two rested a bit, eating their noon meal. "Fill your water jug in case. We're closer than I thought." "River bends a little here and then flows straight to Crossing."

Chapter 36

Old Crossing was the most southern post of the Hudson Bay Company. The community looked large for a settlement so far from any major port. A massive oak tree with overhanging branches stood in the middle, causing the trail to divide on each side of it. "Marks the hunting boundary for the tribes in the area," said River.

Bjorn became anxious. Was Uncle Olaf near here? Did anyone know him? He saw two slanted roof log sheds that had no windows but did have slits on the sides to stick guns through if attacked. Looking down the lane that led to the middle, he spotted two longer and larger sheds. "Furs stored in those?" he asked.

"And whatever else is gotten in trade. Ready to send up the river. Voyageurs usually take the load in their canoes. That hut is the trader's store. Don't know who lives in that one. Inn over there. Let's see if Trader Joe knows anything about Olaf."

Both tied their horses to the railing and entered the store. Four others were seated around the pot belly stove in the middle of the one room log building with a thatched roof. The two windows in front had an oiled cloth rolled above them, used in cold weather to help insulate. Not recognizing any of the four, River went to the counter where Joe sat, watching the men. "Joe, this is Bjorn Hanson. Looking for his uncle. Ever heard of Olaf Seim?"

Trader Joe stood, removed his stocking cap and rubbed his balding head. "Seim. Hmm. Seim. Name seems familiar. Not sure. Person that lives up a ways north of here on the opposite side of the river. Has cows. Brings butter to sell. Eggs too once in a while. Maybe that's him."

"When was he last here?" asked Bjorn.

"Three weeks maybe, not sure."

"We'll stay in the inn if there's room and see if we can find him tomorrow. Need to find Riding Rain. He been around?" River wanted to know.

"Saw him earlier today by one of the warehouses on the other side of the inn. Had moccasins for the Bay Co."

"Thanks," came from both men as they left.

"See if the inn has room. Doesn't seem to be many around or many horses in the lean-to," and he rode towards the open door of the warehouse just on the other side.

In the shadows of early evening, the sod structure River called the inn facing him was about the same size as the store. A prairie schooner sat in front. Looking closer, he saw that sections of the prairie grass were piled one on top of each other to make the walls of the building. The peaked roof was thatched too and the door, made of wood poles, opened easily to a single room. Ropes for beds hung from the ceiling on three sides with a large fireplace built into a stone wall the fourth wall. Mud from the river, grass and dung mixed together, chinked the holes where the uneven rocks and sod left gaping holes.

"Need a bed for the night?" came from a sturdy, woman. A white night cap covered her head and a white apron shielded her long black dress. Heavy leather soled shoes barked as she moved across the floor to him.

"Need two. River'll be here shortly."

"River? He with you? Been waiting for him. Got medicine with him? Cured my rheumatism last time. Back again. So glad. I ache something fierce! You two take those beds against the wall. Bet you haven't slept on boards for a long while, right? Got blankets? Need them, let me know. Stew in the pot. Just made it. Coffee in the other pot. I'll go get Joe. He'll want to know about the trail and the Sioux you've seen," and she spun on her heels and clomped out the door.

Bjorn put his bed roll on the boards that served as a bed on the far side of the hut and sat down to wait for River. The walls had a linen covering that hung from ceiling to floor, white at one time but now stained from the smoke. Two hand hewn tables and as many chairs as would fit around them occupied the center of the room. The fireplace filled one wall and rope beds hung where there was space. The door opened and River entered with the same lady following him in.

"Met Olga, I hear."

"Did," came from her. "Open that bag. Find that rub for my bones. Can't wait. Going to bed early tonight and pile the blankets on. Helped last time. Hope it does this time."

River took his satchel over to the other board bed, removed enough of its contents to get to the bulging coriander seed packet and handed it to her. "Remember what to do with the seeds?"

"Yep. Make a poultice of them. No one else here to sleep. See you in the morning."

"Typical prairie woman. Strong willed like Stone. Soft on the inside."

"Find who you were looking for," asked Bjorn as he ladled two bowls full of the stew left in the pot.

"Did. Medicine bag's pretty empty. Many Pennies is very sick. Took what I had back to Curing Night. He's as good as *Okomisan* is in healing people. Can't find some of the herbs here. Bag was full of them."

"Good stew. Not fish this time. Any idea what the meat is or shouldn't I ask."

"Meat is meat. Herbs change its taste. I can't tell. We'll ride early. Don't know how far up north Olaf may have his holding. Nice to have the place to ourselves."

Bjorn took River's and his bowls, washed both in the basin and set the stew to the edge of the fire to keep warm but not cook away. River spread his bed roll, lay down and was soon asleep. Taking one of the cups handing on the edge of a shelf, Bjorn pored himself coffee, and sat on a stump in front of the fireplace. So close and he was so unsure about this *land of milk and honey* – what it meant for him and what he'd find if he ever found Olaf.

Chapter 37

Bjorn and River woke when the sunlight that streamed through the open door as Olga entered shone directly in their faces. Each rose, got their bedrolls ready and gathered their saddle pouches on the middle of their beds.

"Sleep well? See someone's mama trained one of you right. Thanks. Whoever washed tinware. Making oatmeal and more coffee. Take those out, boys. Get your mounts fed and watered. By that time, I'll have breakfast ready. Know you want to see if you can find that uncle. Olaf? That his name? Don't recall anyone staying here with that name." A continuous flow of words came from Olga as she clanged and banged pots and pans, stirred the fire and added wood to it. When the two returned after stowing their gear and taking care of the horses, she was still talking. "Traded two quilts for an antelope Riding Rain shot. Best meat in the Territory. Feeds off all that green prairie. Not much fat on it. More people come up the trail, looking for land. Lots of it out there. Hard to figure out where one person's land starts and another ends." Bjorn and River finished their biscuits, oatmeal and coffee as quick as they could and took their tinware to the basin. "Leaving so soon? I just got started talking with you. When'll you be back?"

"If I find Olaf, I won't be for a while, I wouldn't think."

"Promised to help Bjorn find his uncle. We'll keep looking. When we find him, I'll head back to Carver's

Cove. *Okomisan* gets worried if I stay away too long. The band continues to make medicine pouches and I'm their trader. I"ll stop when I come through."

"Good food," came from both men as they opened the door and faced the sunshine of a new day.

"Flat land with green waves. That's how I'll explain it to Mor when I write next," mouthed Bjorn.

"I've been as far north as Pembina where the Hudson Bay Company has its post. The trail goes east from there I think. Land doesn't change much from here up to there."

Bjorn kept an eye for changes. Just outside of Old Crossing, he saw the first sod buildings where a family claimed land. A few chickens and two cows were visible. A woman waved from her large garden plot.

A tree or two spawned by seedlings floating in the river and settling on the fertile black shaded the riverbank here and there along the trail. Occasionally a small grove had developed. Area land owners tried to settle in these spots, assured of fuel for their fires and wood for buildings.

A slight bend in the river and a little rise in the land changed the monotonous trail northward. River spotted the homestead first built on a finger of the river. "Bjorn. Suppose that's it? Looks like more than a hut. Built by someone who know wood."

"Ja. Built like some of the *stols* are back home. Might be. Let's go see." He galloped now, so anxious if this truly could be where Olaf lived. When the horses came close, the door opened and a woman, dressed in a long leather dress with symbols of River's people, came out to stand on the step.

River spoke first, using his native language and then he said to Bjorn, "This is Feather. She's been caring for Olaf for a week or more. Heart she thinks."

"Come. Not good. Not long" were the words she offered Bjorn.

Dismounting, Bjorn raced to the entryway and into a separate bedroom where Olaf lay on his board bed. "Olaf. Olaf," he spoke in a reverent, quiet voice. "I'm here. It's Bjorn. Come to live by you."

Slowly, his eyes opened and he reached out his hand to touch the curls around Bjorn's face. "Ja. You. Curls. Little time. Trunk. Letter."

Bjorn turned and saw the trunk up against the opposite wall. Quietly, he walked to it, opened the lid and found a letter addressed to him. Feather and River stood in the doorway, watching. Taking the letter out of the trunk, he moved towards the bed and stopped. "Uncle. Uncle.

No," came in a strained, half-crying voice. "No. I need you. I'm still green." And he shook him, hoping to revive him.

River stepped to the bed, grasped Bjorn's shoulders and held tight until he felt the tension leave Bjorn's body. Bjorn slowly released his hold on the man he'd come to see. "I'll stay and see you through this. Come. Let Feather take care of him.

Chapter 38

Olaf. Gone. Bjorn was devastated. He'd come so far. The letter crushed in his hands; frustration roiled within him. In the lean-to that the livestock shared, River found the pine box Olaf had ready and brought it into the bedroom for Feather who was in the process of washing and dressing Olaf in his Sunday suit.

Feather pointed out the small garden plot in back of the house. Walking back, Bjorn saw a carved cross and went to read the name. Olaf Seim. He'd picked his spot too. River came behind with the shovel and spade and the two began to dig. The two shoveled the heavy black soil in a rhythmic motion, each digging when the other threw his load. About half way to the depth needed, Feather came with bread, meat and milk. The three shared the meal and the digging continued. Measuring with the shovel, Bjorn decided the hole was deep enough and the two returned to the house, carried the box out and placed it in the hole. Bjorn began to recite *"Fader var. . ."* (Our Father . . .). Finishing, he and River covered the box until the garden spot was level again.

Exhausted mentally and physically, Bjorn walked to the lean-to, checked on the stock, and continued down to the river bank where he plopped down on a log. Geese and ducks squawked, frustrated by the intrusion of a human. The river flowed placidly north. River came and quietly sat beside him, allowing him time and space to sort out his feelings and come to terms what the future might mean for him and his dream.

Taking the letter, crumpled and crushed, Bjorn read aloud, knowing River would be anxious too about his future here.

Dear Bjorn,
You are the son I never had. When I read your letter that you were coming, you can't imagine how happy I was. I am so lonesome for anyone from the Old Country. When I wrote your Mor, I hoped you'd decide to come here. I have worked hard to clear land and create a homestead here on the prairie. My heart is not good. It skips beats and sometimes is very slow. I tire easily. I hope I last until you come. All I have will be yours when I die. So that you know what I have, I made a list. Whatever penger *I have will be in the secret drawer in the trunk, like the one I made for your Far. You know where to find it.*

push cart	*2 butcher knives*	*flour barrel*
cradle	*4 sheets*	*bean barrel*
2 hatchets	*2 quilts*	*sugar barrel*
hand saw	*horse blanket*	*oatmeal box*
spade	*2 pillow*	*cornmeal box*
plow	*2 tickings*	*coffee box*
hasp	*2 chairs*	*coffee grinder*
hay knife	*1 rocker*	
pitchfork	*wood bowls*	*10 hens*
hoe	*iron skillet*	*2 roosters*
harrow	*tinware*	*cat*
axe	*4 crocks*	*4 cows*
hammer	*2 wood buckets*	*2 horses*
shovel		*1 bull calf*
wood carving knives	*candles*	
10 pair of wood shoes	*wood carving knives*	
sewing kit	*Bible*	

The land is one of milk and honey but there will be heartache along the way. Stay strong.

Uncle Olaf

Thoughts came jumbling through his mind as he sat. "I have everything I need. Land. Water close. Livestock. Tools. A mansion here in this wild land. River will leave and I'll be alone out here. How will I find someone to share all this with? Who is this Feather that Uncle trusted? What heartaches was Uncle warning me of?" Stone's words of "nothing comes free" rang in his hears. Hungry, he walked back up the trail to the house and entered.

"Feather left a haunch on the spit for us. Bread in the box."
"Where's she?"
"Went back to her people camped along the river north. Leaving in the morning."
"Leaving? Where to?"
"The band goes north from here beyond Pembena. Trapping better there. Feather'd agreed to stay with him until you came."
A sadness different from the death of Olaf overcame Bjorn and he wasn't sure why. "Will the band be back in the spring?"
"Depends on the Sioux. I'll leave in the morning unless you still need me for something."
"I'll need to settle in – whatever that means here. It's up to me to make my dream come true. It'll take me time to adjust. Figure out how green I am. Come when you can. Tell your people they are welcome here at any time." The fireplace embers hardly glowed. Bjorn remained seated in the rocker, sipping the dregs of the coffee. No more was said. No more needed to be. The two thought as one and each knew when morning came he'd miss the other's company.

Map of Journey from Carver's Cove to Old Crossing

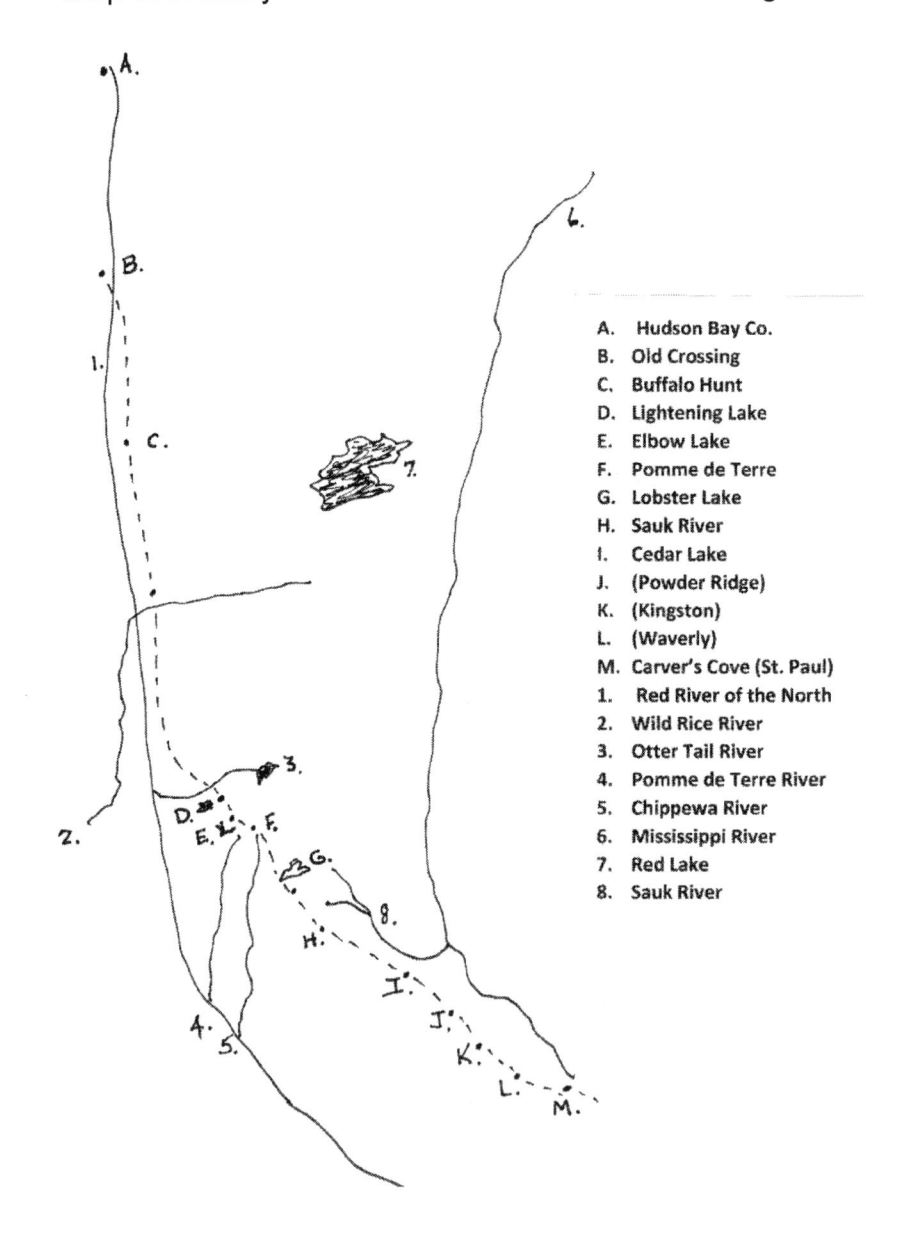

A. Hudson Bay Co.
B. Old Crossing
C. Buffalo Hunt
D. Lightening Lake
E. Elbow Lake
F. Pomme de Terre
G. Lobster Lake
H. Sauk River
I. Cedar Lake
J. (Powder Ridge)
K. (Kingston)
L. (Waverly)
M. Carver's Cove (St. Paul)
1. Red River of the North
2. Wild Rice River
3. Otter Tail River
4. Pomme de Terre River
5. Chippewa River
6. Mississippi River
7. Red Lake
8. Sauk River

Other Books by Jan Smith

Norse Trollology Series

Crossing the Arctic – Book 1
A Norse Fjell Troll Story

Fy and Aina – Book 2
A New World Love Story

Historical Fiction:

Homesteading the Land
Phelps Mill – 1890

Remembering the *Maine*
Riding with Roosevelt – 1898

Website: storiesandyou.com

Synopsis of Norse Troll books written by Jan Smith:

Crossing the Arctic
A Norse Fjell Troll Story
Book 1

Crossing the Arctic is the story of a Norse Fjell Trollet, a mountain troll. Ridiculed because of his lack of cleanliness, Fy decides to follow in his father's footsteps and make his way from Norway to the **New World** in order to start a new life for himself. Receded fjord waters impacted by glacial movement and ice jams in the Arctic allow Fy to take advantage of his huge height and *walk* across. Two Nisse, small Norse troll people, accompany him and the three face adventures on the journey to the **New World**.

FY and Aina
A New World Love Story
Book 2

Aina loves salmon, needs to replenish her supply and goes fishing. Ocean waves capsize her boat. Fy hears someone pleading for help and swims out to rescue the person, and discovers he's saved a Norse Fjell trollet like himself. **Fy and Aina** is the story of their meeting, the adventures they share with the Nisse in the mountainous area, and the companionship they discover as they spend time together.

Synopsis of Historical Fiction books written by Jan Smith:

Homesteading the Land
Phelps Mill - 1890

The story is set in Otter Tail County in the **Phelps Mill** area known then as Maine, Minnesota. Arriving by prairie schooner, living in a tent, building a sod house and finally a log home, each become adventures for Nivek. Almost daily visits to the mill delivering lunch, to McConkey's store, school and farming, fishing and hunting (sometimes with the neighbor boys) become "lessons in life." **Homesteading the Land** is a fictional look at the daily life of a land-claiming family of five in the year 1890. Many of the characters, events and places, however, allude to *actual local people and happenings* of that year. *197 pages – author illustrated*

Remembering the Maine
Riding with Roosevelt

Remembering the Maine continues the story of the young Nivek James, introduced in the previous book **Homesteading the Land**. Leaving his family homestead in Minnesota, he becomes a newspaper correspondent during the Spanish-American War, 1898. With his boyhood friends, Wing, an Ojibwa Indian, and Jesse, from Medora, North Dakota, the young men travel across country by horseback, train, and stagecoach on their journey to join the Rough Riders and Theodore Roosevelt. This book is the story of their journey, the training of the troops, and the war in Cuba. It is a coming-of-age tale of bravery, courage, hardships and patriotism set against the background of emergence of the U.S.A. as a world power. Nivek's dispatches to the **Minnesota News** give a personal account of the times. *201 pages – author illustrated*

ORDERING BOOKS

- Place order on website:
  storiesandyou.com

CONTACT THE AUTHOR

Website: storiesandyou.com